HUNTRESS SCOUT

HUNTRESS CLAN SAGA™ BOOK 4

JAMIE DAVIS

LMBPN

DISRUPTIVE IMAGINATION

LMBPN Publishing
PMB 196, 2540 South Maryland Pkwy
Las Vegas, NV 89109

First US Edition, May, 2020
eBook ISBN: 978-1-64202-913-0
Print ISBN: 978-1-64202-914-7

HUNTRESS SCOUT

THE HUNTRESS SCOUT TEAM

Thanks to the JIT Readers

Dave Hicks
Diane L. Smith
Deb Mader
John Ashmore
Kerry Mortimer
Larry Omans
Jeff Goode

If I've missed anyone, please let me know!

Editor
The Skyhunter Editing Team

The breath whooshed out of Quinn's lungs as the other woman's fist drove into her solar plexus. Doubling over, Quinn twisted to the side, using the downward momentum to roll left and bounce back to her feet. She gasped to catch her breath.

Damn, she was fast. Too fast.

Her opponent's dark hair was pulled back in a ponytail. The woman smiled, her fangs showing. "Is that all you've got? This is going to be easier than I thought."

As Quinn straightened, the drained stamina bar flashed red in her HUD. The boosted speed and strength flowed from her. She tried to hide the loss of her temporary advantage as the other woman squared up opposite her.

The vampire blurred, moving so fast, Quinn had trouble following her. Somehow, though, Quinn blocked all the incoming strikes, batting aside blows from hands and feet coming in complex combinations she'd never seen before. It was like trying to fight a tornado swirling around her.

There was no way she could keep it up.

Quinn didn't know how to quit. She fought on, even without any strength left. It wasn't like she had a choice. The damned vampire showed no sign of slowing.

At last, a kick at her ankles connected. Quinn hopped a little too late to avoid the sweep, and it knocked her legs out from beneath her.

A shout of triumph sounded from the other woman as Quinn toppled over and crashed to the unforgiving stone floor. The vampire followed her exultant cheer with a laugh. She bent down, exposing her extended canines, ready to clamp down on her prey.

Quinn tried to roll away from the other woman, but she had landed astride the Huntress. She pinned Quinn's arms to the floor above her head.

The vampire leaned forward, bringing her fangs down to Quinn's neck.

She whispered in Quinn's ear, her cool undead breath tickling a little as she spoke. "You're dead."

"Enough!" Clark yelled.

Naomi sat up, still kneeling astride Quinn's waist. "She's not fast enough, Clark. Without some external source of power, her reserves run dry too quickly to maintain her in a fight against anyone with real skill."

"Get off!" Quinn said, pushing at Naomi's thighs so she could get up. With her strength sapped, she couldn't budge the other woman.

Clark came over as Naomi stood and stepped to the side so Quinn could rise. He looked down. "She's right, Quinn. You've been using things like ley lines and other outside magical reinforcement as a crutch. That's my fault for letting you get away with it."

"I've done just fine so far. I've saved you both—twice now for Clark, I might add."

Naomi let out a mocking laugh. "I've survived all these years when no one thought I could. You almost died twice in that chamber against John Handon. If I hadn't remembered the legends of the past clan leaders watching over the rest of us and pointed it out to you, you'd be a vampire, and we'd both be servants of John Handon right now."

"I would have figured it out on my own. The spirits in that room spoke to me before you thought of it."

Naomi scoffed and turned aside. She walked to the wooden table nearby, picking up a bag of fresh blood and sipping from it like it was a juice box.

Quinn pointed to her opponent. "She has a lot of nerve telling me I draw on external energy too much. Look at her refilling her reserves over there. It's not fair."

"No," Clark barked at her. "It's not. None of this is fair. You're always going to be outnumbered, overpowered, and fighting from a disadvantage. Get used to it. The rest of the clans are gone, so no one else is going to come in and help you. You've got to find a way to build your internal reserves, Quinn. You might not like it, but your mother's right."

"Don't call her that," Quinn snapped.

Naomi flinched at the vehemence of the reply, a fact not missed by Quinn.

Deep inside, part of her regretted saying it, but in her current anger at both Clark and Naomi, she brushed it aside. She still struggled to adjust to having her mother around again. Quinn's deep-seated emotional wounds from a difficult childhood in foster care did little to resolve her conflicted feelings.

Naomi put the blood bag down and pointed at the plastic jug of water and cups beside it on the table. "Come over and drink something. Then we'll try it again."

"What's the point? I'm dry. My stamina is drained, so there's no way I can match your speed and strength."

"The point, my dear daughter, is that you've got to find a way to power through when that happens. We somehow need to supplement your stamina from within or learn how to increase how much you can store."

"She's right, Quinn. Drink some water while I think of some way to get you to do what any norm—" Clark stopped and didn't finish the sentence.

"What? You were going to say I can't do what a normal Huntress could do?" Quinn stared at Naomi. "I missed out on the training any other clan member would've had. There's no fixing it, so that option's out. I'll never get that back, so it's useless to even mention it."

Quinn forced her clenched fists to relax and walked over to the table, where she poured herself some water. The cool liquid soothed her parched throat. As she drank and refilled the cup, she stared around the vaulted underground chamber. The walls, lined with carefully cut blocks of granite, had become their new home base. Since she'd vanquished the vampire John Handon and his followers, they'd moved their clan's home to the tunnels attached to the back of O'Malley's supernatural bar in East Baltimore.

She ran her fingers through her sweat-soaked hair and

downed the second cupful of water. They'd been at this training session for over two hours this morning. Part of her short temper had to do with her exhaustion and dehydration. Realizing Naomi had once again proven to be right brought her quelled anger back.

Naomi raised a hand to rest on Quinn's shoulder, but her daughter pulled away. Letting it drop to her side, she said, "You've accomplished more than I would have thought, Quinn. I need to remember that while we're training you. Plus, you can do things no other Hunter has ever been able to do. Pulling energy from ley lines and other power sources for anything other than a few small spells or healing is completely new."

"But it's not good enough. You just said so."

Naomi shook her head. "I was wrong to say it that way. You've done so much on your own, but I believe you have to find a way to work on your skills without drawing on external sources of power. If you can do that, you'll be much more likely to survive a tough fight, especially against someone who could find a way to block any power source."

"They can do that?" Quinn asked.

Clark nodded. "Naomi knows what she's talking about. If they figure out what you are doing, a powerful sorcerer might come up with a way to sever your connection to the ley lines. I don't think it would be easy, I'd have to check with Miranda about that one, but it's possible. Even if it drained or injured the caster, if it kept you from using the energy, it would be worth the effort if it hobbled your ability to defend yourself."

Naomi smiled and said, "The good news is that

somehow that VR system Taylor made and the magic infused into it have given you a way to learn things and add skills you didn't have. That gives me hope that we can get you caught up with the Hunter training you missed."

"I'm not just an ordinary Hunter, Naomi. I'm a Huntress. I'm building something new and different."

"You keep saying that, but what does that mean?" Naomi asked. "We've had women Hunters before you. I was one."

Quinn shook her head. "I don't know for sure. I just know that as soon as I first said it, somehow it felt right. It's like when the last puzzle piece fits into place and completes the picture. I can't see the whole thing yet, but I have a feeling I was the final piece to start something that has been waiting a long time for me."

Clark smiled. "You may be right, Quinn. I've certainly seen you do things I didn't think were possible. But that's all the more reason for you to do everything you can do to explore your powers and see if you can stretch beyond the ones we know about. That's all Naomi and I are trying to do."

Naomi nodded. "Maybe this is enough combat training for now. Let's mix it up and try something different. It's possible we can jar loose another sort of Hunter skill."

"What are you thinking?" Clark asked.

"We've got some time before you two normally eat lunch. I'm thinking our girl here could use some scout training. You said she has tracking skills. Let's see if she can track me."

"Perfect," Clark said. "But won't we have to wait until dark? You'll sizzle outside at this time of day."

"Not outside," Naomi said. "Here, down in the maze."

Quinn didn't know what "the maze" was, but she didn't like the grin spreading across Clark's face.

The two instructors left the training chamber, with Quinn trailing behind them.

CHAPTER TWO

Quinn Faust stared down the long stone passageway. Even in the relative darkness, the careful placement of the carved stone blocks showed an old-world craftsmanship you didn't see much in the modern world. Clark and Naomi had led her down a tunnel off the main Hunters' ceremonial chamber. It sloped downward until it reached this long corridor.

She turned to Clark. "So, what? I just go down there and try to find her in these catacombs? What is that supposed to teach me?"

Clark frowned and shook his head. "It's called the maze, and your mother was right about you needing to catch up in your training. This is a different sort of skill to build on."

"I told you, don't call her my mother. She birthed me, that's all."

"I won't argue with you." Clark shook his head. "That's something you need to settle with Naomi. It doesn't change what we want you to do here."

Quinn gave a small nod at his use of the woman's

name instead of the other word. "I just don't see the point. I've done well enough, and we've been training all morning. The skills I have serve well enough. They did the trick when we took out Handon and his vampire goons."

"You know as well as I do that was luck as much as anything. You won't always get a boost from nearby spirits to bolster your power. This is to help hone your inherent abilities. They're in there, within you. Naomi and I think we can jar them loose by putting you through some specific training scenarios. This one is to teach you to use your other senses to detect when supernatural creatures are nearby."

"I can already detect werewolves and other shifters. I can smell them when they get close. What am I supposed to smell when I get near a vampire?"

Clark smiled. "I can't describe it to you, Quinn. You have your own unique way of doing this. You can already do different things than I could at your stage. You have to discover how those abilities work for you, not how I learned it. Now, Naomi is down there. It's always been called the maze by everyone I ever heard talk about it. You'll see why once you go down there. Find her if you can. She's not going to make it easy, so don't let your guard down. I'll wait up here. Once you find her, come back, and then we'll go and grab some lunch."

Quinn's stomach grumbled at the mention of food. She and Clark had been training all morning, and she'd worked up a huge appetite.

Clark chuckled at the sound of her churning gut. "Better get going. If you take too long, I'll head up to eat lunch without you. Naomi just fed, so she won't care if it takes you all day to find her."

Quinn clenched her teeth and bit back another complaint. Clark was right. Naomi would take great pleasure in stretching this exercise to fill the whole day. The former-Hunter-turned-vampire didn't have anywhere to be until after dark.

Walking forward, Quinn muttered under her breath, "Dammit, I need to see." In an instant, the darkness around her took on a greenish tint, and the whole passageway brightened. With her Huntress night vision enabled, Quinn began her search.

The passage branched in several directions a little way along from her position, with each branch dividing further. These tunnels had been built by the Hunter clan here in Baltimore early in the city's history. When Quinn asked what they were for, Clark and Naomi both shrugged and said, "Training."

It seemed like a lot of work for a training course. They could've accomplished more with an above-ground setup. The twisting maze made no sense at all. Sometimes the tunnels opened up, with side passages branching straight up into the ceiling. Other times, there were pits and tunnel openings in the floor she had leap over.

An hour later, Quinn stopped at an intersection with another passageway and tried to decide if she should come up with a better plan. She still didn't understand how she was supposed to find Naomi. For all she knew, the vampire wasn't even down here. Clark could have cooked up a fake hunt to test her.

Quinn concentrated, and a faint map overlay appeared

in front of her eyes, just like in the HUD in a video game. The blinking dot showed her location, and as she traced the twisting tunnels on the map, she cursed. She'd traveled this part of the course before.

Thinking back to what Clark said at the beginning of the test, Quinn realized she needed a new approach. She hadn't found the vampire hiding as she searched, and that probably meant Naomi had moved to stay ahead of her. Recalling Clark's earlier instructions, the Huntress considered the different ways she could track someone. The initial tracking skill she'd gained from the VR system didn't seem to work with vampires. Maybe it could only track the living.

Quinn focused on her five senses. She'd been using her eyes, and that wasn't working. With shifters, she could smell when they were nearby, especially werewolves. Their distinctive wet-dog scent was hard to miss. She wondered what a vampire would smell like.

Quinn closed her eyes and flared her nostrils, drawing a deep breath, taking in the various smells around her in this underground tunnel system. Odors of earth and a faint dusty mustiness filled her nostrils. She took another breath, concentrating the same way she did when opening her HUD, trying to meld her sense of smell with her Huntress abilities like she had with shifters. This time a vague hint of another scent reached her. Her nose wrinkled when she realized it was the odor of death and decay.

Turning her head, Quinn sniffed the air in the direction of the branching side tunnels. She picked up more of the scent from the opening to her right, so she opened her eyes and started up that tunnel.

The scent grew stronger, and she picked up speed. The passage angled to the left up ahead and Quinn ran forward, sure her prey lay just around that bend. She turned the corner at a dead run.

A leg extended from a hidden crack in the wall, tripping her. She tumbled to the paving stones, skidding on her chest along the floor.

Quinn recovered and tucked her shoulder as she slid, allowing her to roll back to her feet. She drew her Bowie knife as she rolled and popped up, holding it out in front of her, ready to defend herself.

Naomi stepped from the shadows of a hidden space in the wall. She pointed to the weapon in Quinn's left hand. "Put that away unless you want to spar."

Quinn glanced down at her knife and returned it to the sheath nestled beneath her right armpit. "Have you been here the whole time? I checked this passage at least one other time."

"Twice, actually," Naomi said. "I was tempted to jump you the second time you passed, but I realized you hadn't detected me; you were just wandering around trusting you'd get lucky. This time, you moved with purpose. You figured it out, didn't you?"

Quinn nodded. She sniffed the air again. The faint odor of decay was stronger now that Naomi stood only a few feet away. "How come I don't smell you all the time?"

Naomi shrugged. "You should be able to. I could before I was turned. Learning the different smells of common supernatural creatures was something taught to me while I was learning to read and write. It should become second nature to you once you match a smell to a particular creature."

Wondering about that, Quinn concentrated on the display only she could see. Right away, she spotted a new triangular icon appearing where her other skills showed up as she activated them. She shook her head. "I don't think it's there all the time. It just popped up as a new ability in my HUD."

Naomi smiled. "I wish I could see what that looks like. I envy you the ability to gain skills that way. It should make it easier in theory. At least there's a way to reach into your dormant abilities and activate them somehow. You should be happy. This is a move in a positive direction, Quinn. Clark and I have been struggling with ways to get you to open up that hidden part of yourself."

The vampire reached out to lay her hand on her daughter's shoulder. Quinn stepped back, avoiding the gesture.

Naomi withdrew her hand and dropped her arm to her side.

Quinn didn't miss the frown or the sadness in the other woman's eyes. Looking away from Naomi, she said, "Come on, Clark'll be waiting at the maze's entrance. He's probably annoyed I took this long to find you. Besides, I need to eat something."

Naomi nodded and the pair returned to the central hall. Neither of them said anything as they walked, and the silence weighed on Quinn. Naomi had made several overtures to show affection and try to get Quinn to open up. Each time, as in the training course just now, Quinn moved to resist contact. In a few instances, she left the room.

Conflicting emotions warred within her. The hurt of

learning her mother had always been there, watching her from a distance most nights without telling Quinn she was alive warred with the joy of discovering she wasn't alone. That joy had been magnified when Naomi agreed to join the newly-formed Huntress clan. Conflicting emotions roiled beneath the surface and kept Quinn from returning the affection her mother showed from time to time.

Clark sat waiting on a stone bench inside the Hunters' ceremonial chamber as the two women emerged from the maze. He stroked the sharpening stone in one last pass across his short sword before returning it to his pocket, then laid the sword across his knees and looked up.

"Took you long enough. The course isn't that big. You should have found her sooner."

"I found her, that's all you need to worry about. I also discovered a new ability popped up in the display I see sometimes. I should be able to track other kinds of super-naturals now once I've met them and learned their scents."

Clark smiled. "I'd hoped you could unlock that in some way ever since you detected Handon's werewolves outside his office building. I'll try to make it so you meet other sorts of creatures and build up a list of things you can detect."

"Sounds good to me. Now, can we please go up to O'Malley's and get some lunch?"

"Yeah, sure. I don't know why it took you so long to ask." Clark laughed and sheathed his sword. The three of them headed toward the stairs leading up to the bar and their new accommodations.

Paddy O'Malley, the leprechaun who owned the hidden bar serving supernaturals, smiled as the three of them entered. A pretty decent lunch crowd came in each day from among the locals who worked in the area.

The jolly owner came over and said, "Goodness, Quinn, my girl, what did they do to you down there?"

Quinn realized her sweat-matted hair from earlier had dried in a less than complimentary style. She combed her hair with her fingers to try to tame it a little. A lot had fallen out of her ponytail, and she pulled off the elastic band and gathered her long dark hair again in a fresh one.

Clark came to the rescue. "Just a little training, Paddy. We're all ready for some lunch now, though."

Paddy glanced at Naomi. "All of you?"

"I'm fine," Naomi said. "I had a snack down there. Just some beer for me."

"Ah, beer, I can do." A big grin spread across his face as he called to his daughter Juni, seating a group at a table nearby. "A table for our esteemed guests, girl. Quick, before they pass out from hunger and thirst."

"We're fine, Paddy," Clark said. The three of them headed over to where Juni waved them to a table near the bar.

"Don't pay any attention to him," she said as she handed them menus. "He's all bluster. He knows full well I run this place. Now, what'll you have to drink while you check out our specials?"

"Soda for Quinn. Pick something nice on tap for Naomi and me."

"Will do. Be right back."

Juni headed back to the bar to get their drinks. Clark glanced at Quinn. "So, what did she smell like?"

"Huh?" Quinn asked, a little confused.

"She's half-leprechaun. You should be able to pick up something. You definitely should've gotten a scent from Paddy."

Quinn shook her head. "It doesn't work that way for me, I don't think. I have to activate it first to use it, like in a video game. I'll try again when she comes back."

Naomi smiled. "That must be pretty cool, having a game inside your head all the time like that."

"I guess so." Quinn shrugged. "Sometimes it gives me a splitting headache, especially if I leave the HUD up too long. I think it's because of the differences between the real world compared to being inside the VR system. In there, it's more natural and feels like everything is real. Out here, I have to concentrate hard to bring up the display and do anything."

Juni came back with a tray holding their drinks. Quinn brought up her HUD and clicked on the new triangle icon with her mind. When the short waitress came over to set down her soda, Quinn took in a deep breath.

The scent of new-mown grass and something like hot breakfast tea drifted into her nasal passages. As Juni pulled out her pad to take their lunch order, Quinn grinned and gave her companions a brief nod. Naomi and Clark returned her grin.

"What'll it be?" Juni asked.

"I'll have a burger, fries, and add a bowl of the cream of crab soup, please," Quinn said.

"That sounds good," Clark said. "I'll have the same."

"Good to go. I'll be back with your meal in a little bit. Flag me down if you need refills on those drinks." Juni took the stacked menus and left.

"You got it?" Naomi asked.

"She smelled like a freshly cut lawn and tea. Is that right?"

Clark and Naomi both shrugged, and Quinn was confused. Clark picked up on her facial expression and said, "My understanding is it's different for each Hunter—or Huntress."

"What does she smell like to you?" Quinn asked.

"Aged Irish whiskey." Clark glanced at Naomi.

"Don't look at me," Naomi said. That part of me isn't working anymore. All I can smell is the blood coursing through her veins. It makes me wonder what leprechaun tastes like."

"Ewww," Quinn said. "She's a friend."

Naomi dismissed Quinn's comment with a wave of her hand. "Don't worry. I don't feed on anyone who isn't willing. Besides, I think our host would be angry if I bit his daughter."

"That reminds me," Quinn said, turning to Clark. "How long is he going to let us use the apartments above the bar?"

"If he knows what's good for him, he'll let us stay indefinitely. He claims not to have been aware of what really happened with Handon and his minions down below. I don't believe him, and he knows it. As long as that's the case, I'm inclined to soak him for all the free food, drink, and lodging he's got."

Naomi nodded and pointed behind Quinn. "Speaking of lodging, here come Taylor and Miranda."

Quinn greeted her friends. They'd just entered the bar via the door beside the kitchen that led up to the apartments above the bar. The previous residents had been members of John Handon's VirSync cultist followers. They were all dead now and didn't need the rooms, so Clark had suggested to Paddy that he let the clan move in.

"Pull up a chair," the Huntress called to her best friend.

Taylor smiled and walked over, the ghostly form of Miranda the witch drifting across the floor behind her.

"How'd the training go this morning?" Taylor asked as she sat down.

"Fine, I guess," Quinn replied. She didn't think it had gone that well.

"She's being modest," Naomi said with more excitement than Quinn expected from her. "She unlocked a new skill, and without using the VR system. I think that is a break-through."

"That's great," Taylor said. "That means I can dismantle some of the rig I made and make some tweaks I've been meaning to add. Miranda and I have been discussing the unique Hunter spells we found in the *Life Tome*. We think we can use them to enhance your experience inside the VR system and maybe juice up your stamina score. You'd be able to hold more at one time."

Clark snapped his fingers. "That's exactly what we need. How long will it take?"

"It depends on how much I need to tweak it as it installs. The question is, can I start now, or do we have to wait?"

"This is probably a good time to do it," Quinn said. "Things have been quiet for the first month or so since we took care of Handon's vampires and cultists. What do you think?" She turned to Clark.

The old Hunter shrugged. "Things have settled down in the city for the most part. There are some disappearances on the south side of town I've been keeping an eye on, but I suppose we can take a chance and shut it down for a few days."

Taylor smiled. "Excellent. I'll start in on it later today. We have a few more things in the *Tome* to investigate before we begin the rebuild."

Naomi said, "If you're going through the Clan spells and rituals, I might be able to help. I still want to see if there's a way to make up for all the training Quinn missed growing up. She's doing very well, but there are giant holes in her knowledge and abilities."

The statement irked Quinn. "I'll remind everyone you both just said I did very well this morning."

"It's like you're working with a half-empty toolbox," Naomi said. "If you had all the things you were missing, you'd find it much easier to complete all the additional training we want to do with you."

"You and Clark had all that growing up," Quinn said. "You act like you're doing all this blind sometimes."

Clark shook his head. "I was just an initiate when the purges happened. There was a lot I had to teach myself. It took me years, and I still can't do all the things I'd like, not like a Master Hunter used to be able to do."

"And I lost touch with the magical Hunter enhancements when I was turned into a vampire," Naomi added. "I kept my martial skills and enhanced strength and speed. My vampire side even adds to that side of things, but I can't use most of the Hunter skills I learned growing up."

"And the two of you complain about how *I'm* doing,"

Quinn said under her breath. She shook her head, letting out a wry chuckle. "It figures."

"That's not fair, Quinn," Miranda chastised. "You're better than that. Both of them are doing the best they can. On top of that, they're the only resource we have. You should be grateful you can access any of their knowledge."

Quinn didn't feel like apologizing, although she knew that was what the ghost wanted. No one here understood the pressure the training and everyone's expectations put on her. Three times now, when everything went into the crapper, she'd been the one to bail them all out. Couldn't they give her a break and try to see it from her side?

Taylor came to Quinn's rescue like she'd done so many times when stress started to overwhelm her. "Hey, did you all order already? I'm starving. Should I track down Juni?"

Clark took the hint and nodded. "We did. I'll go get her. Do you need a menu?"

"No." Taylor shook her head. "Tell her I'll have the pizza burger and a side of Old Bay fries."

After Clark left to find Juni, Taylor glanced at Quinn and smiled. Quinn nodded and mouthed, "Thank you."

Miranda shifted gears and started talking to Naomi about old Baltimore landmarks from years ago, including some sort of concert club called Hammerjack's. Quinn had never heard of it, but from the animated way the two talked about it, it must've been quite the hot spot.

Happy to be out from under the spotlight of the conversation, Quinn sat back and listened to the others chatter about random things for the rest of lunch.

CHAPTER THREE

aylor sat down behind the desk in the makeshift
office Paddy had set up for her in one of his storerooms. The light in there sucked and it smelled slightly
sour, but the room wasn't all bad. She had power and
plenty of room, and she was able to tap directly into one of
the cable company's data lines, so she had super-fast internet. The conduit ran through the tunnel outside.

Miranda floated over to the opposite side of the desk
and assumed a sitting position so she was at Taylor's level.
"Where were we?" she asked, pointing at the computer
screens.

Taylor tapped the touchpad, lighting up the triple
monitors arrayed next to her. The displays filled with color
scans of the pages of the ancient Hunter book they'd stolen
and copied. It was in Latin, but Taylor had used an app
from a friend to translate the flowing handwritten script
into English. The translation for each page hovered in a
window superimposed over each page.

She pointed to the left-hand screen. "I'm intrigued by the description of this spell."

Miranda leaned over and scanned the screen while Taylor scrolled through the script.

"See, it's some sort of enhancement spell used on Hunter children as they trained to imprint certain skills and abilities on them. I don't see why this couldn't be used to do something similar with Quinn in the VR system. This part refers to magical power, doesn't it?"

Miranda shook her head. "That spell borders on dark magic. I wouldn't cast it on anyone, especially not a child. This would be like playing with a person's genetic sequence without knowing exactly what the effects would be."

"But it's clear in the description it was used all the time on younglings in training," Taylor said. Her finger traced the section of the text that said as much. "It must've worked, or they wouldn't have used it."

"Oh, I'm sure it works…most of the time. What about the times it didn't take or had an unintentional side effect? This spell could just as easily manifest in a skill not unlike the life-draining effect of a demon or a ghoul. That wouldn't meet the Hunter code."

"You think that happened?"

"I think it happened often enough that we would have heard about it unless they did something with the failures."

"Wait," Taylor said. "You think they killed the Hunter children who didn't react to the spell as expected? That's awful."

Miranda nodded. "The Hunter clans kept apart from the others in the supernatural community, but there've always been rumors about the harshness of their training methods and of trainees who died in the process of becoming Hunters. This is probably an example of how that could happen. I'd be willing to bet it's not the only spell of the sort we're going to find."

"I was hoping this could be a way to help Quinn catch up to where Clark and Naomi think she should be. I don't think they see the effect her frequent failures have on her competitive nature. She doesn't have an ounce of quit in her. She won't stop pushing herself until she completes a task or a training session."

Miranda nodded. "I've seen it. Clark has, too. He's mentioned it to me on more than one occasion. The problem might be that he sees it as a positive thing."

Taylor snorted and rolled her eyes. "He would."

"He's not entirely wrong, Taylor. What she's learning to do, to be, isn't easy. You'd all have been dead, like me, long ago if she wasn't like that. I just hope he tempers his methods with an eye toward letting her have a win from time to time. She can't always have a breakthrough like she had today."

"I can't tell whose side you're on."

"Quinn's, ours. The whole clan's, I guess." Miranda spread her arms wide. "Dealing with the energy and magic, the supernatural creatures, all of this, it isn't easy or for the faint at heart. The same is true for those who learn to be mages. Not everyone makes it through the process."

"People die?" Taylor asked. "I seem to have adapted well enough."

"You had more aptitude than most, and you had the supplemental strength of your werewolf side to help you manage the stress on your body from handling the raw energy. Think of it like this: harnessing magical energy is like wiring a live high-voltage circuit to a transformer without any safety gear. It's possible to do it without electrocuting yourself, but one mistake, one tiny slip, and you're dead."

Taylor blanched. "Why didn't you tell me that when you taught me to cast the spells for the VR system interface?"

"Because you were already trying to teach yourself. That was far more dangerous. You wouldn't have stopped, even if I had told you. All it would've done was to make you nervous and self-conscious. You didn't need the distraction while you were mastering the process. We didn't have the time to take things slowly."

"Gee, thanks," Taylor said. She smiled as she thought about it. "You're right, though. I'm a little like Quinn in that regard. I get tunnel vision when I'm working on a project and miss the possible consequences."

Taylor turned back to the screen. "Let's put this one aside for a while and see what else might be helpful. Quinn needs us to find a win for her."

The two of them dug in and started going through the list of spells and rituals Taylor had made that might be useful. It took them the rest of the day, but they boiled it all down to three potential additions. One would enable Quinn to see magical energy in the world and maybe store it in some way. She might even be able to manipulate it for simple spells.

Another might give her limited healing abilities. Quinn would be able to channel health energy, either to help others with their injuries or to regenerate injuries of her own. She had already used direct energy from ley lines to recharge her Huntress powers and stamina. This would let her channel the magic around her and her reserves, transforming it into healing energy for another person. There was mention in the *Tome* that Hunters in the past could do that.

The final option Miranda and Taylor discovered was the riskiest of the three because of the dark magic it employed. The two of them had argued about it for some time before Miranda relented and admitted it was worth taking the chance. It wasn't really a spell. It was a ritual that merged the dark magic used in demonic possession with Quinn's Huntress powers.

If it was successful, she should be able to detect demons who were close by, including those humans possessed by demonic souls as demon-kinder. It might even allow Quinn to see dark magical energy around her and enable detection of traps or detection spells cast by her opponents.

The risk was substantial, however, so they decided to leave it for last. Miranda believed if they messed up the ritual for that one, it would make her more susceptible to demonic magic and influence, not more resistant.

When they were finished, Taylor smiled and said, "I think we can get started on the first upgrade tomorrow."

"So soon?" Miranda asked. "Don't you want to study the spells and practice first?"

Taylor shrugged. "I don't think so. I can already recite the necessary parts of the spell that won't be coded into the system. It'll require more time to take apart the VR system components and make the adjustments needed to upgrade things. We found that cache of the new VirSync equipment in one of O'Malley's storerooms. I want to swap them out for the parts I built from scratch. Those are the weak points in our setup.

"How long will it be down if you do that? You told Clark two days. Any longer, and we might need it," Miranda said.

"Two days should be right, especially if we leave off that last upgrade. Between us, we've already mastered how to get the VR system working with our gear. This is just adding improvements and professionally designed equipment to what we already have."

Miranda nodded. "Fair enough. I'll be here first thing in the morning so we can get started fresh. I'm a little tired right now. I've been manifesting in the corporeal world a lot over the last week. I need to take the night off."

"You've been able to stay longer each time, though. That's an improvement."

"It is, but it also makes it so I need more downtime in between. Don't worry. Tonight should be enough rest. I'll see you tomorrow."

Taylor nodded as Miranda faded from view. She stared at the space where the ghost had hovered moments before. Taylor wondered if the witch was still here and just unable to be seen or to speak. That would be creepy unless she went somewhere else when she faded out. Taylor made a mental note to ask her ghostly friend next time she saw her.

Realizing she'd grown tired, too, Taylor shut down her systems and locked her screens before heading out of her storeroom-office. The door had a lock that Taylor used, but she had no idea how many others had a key beside Paddy and her. Best to make sure her systems were secured from random hacking in case someone got inside.

Humming to herself, Taylor headed back down the passage toward the rear entrance to the bar. The others would probably already be there ordering dinner. She was starving and needed meat to feed her wolf side.

CHAPTER FOUR

Two days later, Quinn flopped down on her bed, letting out a long sigh at finally getting to rest her weary muscles. For the last forty-eight hours, Clark had left the training regimen to Naomi while he made his rounds in the city to check on the supernatural community. He didn't say why, only that there were some potential trouble spots he wanted to look in on.

Quinn had hoped Taylor would have finished her VR system upgrades today. She could've used it as an excuse for a break from the non-stop practice bouts and exercises Naomi ran for her. Quinn hated to admit it, but the vampire made Clark's brand of harsh training methods look like nursery school playtime by comparison.

Quinn rolled over to stare at the ceiling. She groaned as her muscles protested the move. "Ugh, I wish Taylor wasn't tied up with the VR rig. I could use someone to talk to right now."

She caught a bit of movement out of the corner of her eye, but when she turned to see what it was, all she saw was a stack of her laundry topped with the football-sized dragon egg she'd ended up with after their foiled raid on Princess Aurora's compound over a month before.

Swinging her legs over the side of the bed and sitting up, Quinn reached out and lifted the polished green egg from the pile of folded clothes and set it in her lap. It was always a bit warmer than the ambient temperature, and sometimes she swore she could detect an occasional faint tremor or vibration from within when holding it.

"You have it easy, my little friend. You get to just hang out and do nothing all day. No one expects anything from you."

Quinn stared down at the egg and laughed. "Fine, don't say anything. I see how you are."

She set the egg down on her pillow and got up to gather some underwear and a nightshirt for after her shower. The hot water splashing on her aching muscles and bruises would make everything better.

Quinn glanced over her shoulder as she headed for her bedroom door. "Coming?" She said to the egg on her pillow. "The steamy heat might feel good."

The best thing about their move to O'Malley's was that everyone got their own apartment in the two buildings situated above the underground club and passages. Quinn's was next to Taylor's in the converted row home adjacent to the club's alley entrance.

Hitting the bathroom, she took a long shower. She'd swung the door shut but not latched and the space filled with steam, fogging up the mirror and creating a warm cloud across the top half of the bathroom.

Sliding the shower curtain back, Quinn grabbed her

towel and stepped out as she started to dry off. She took a step toward the fogged mirror over the sink and stubbed her toe on something, cursing aloud.

"Dammit, what the…"

Quinn stopped as she stared down at the tile floor. The dragon egg rocked in place from when she'd kicked it by accident. How had it gotten in?

She glanced up and saw the bathroom door was now ajar.

Someone was inside her apartment.

Wrapping the towel around her torso and tucking in the end to hold it in place, Quinn calculated the distance to the kitchen counter where she'd left her shoulder holster rig and her Bowie knife.

If an intruder waited in the hallway outside, they'd likely catch up with her before she could dash out and get to her weapon. Of course, she wasn't completely helpless. Calling up her stamina in the HUD, she saw the bar had filled up some since she'd depleted it in her earlier training sessions.

Drawing on the small amount she'd recovered, Quinn boosted her speed and strength and yanked the door open. With a bound, expecting to be tackled from behind at any moment, she darted down the hallway for the kitchen.

Her towel came loose and dropped to the floor as she ran. She was stark naked when she grabbed at the hilt of her Bowie and spun around to face her attacker.

There was no one there.

Quinn glanced down self-consciously but didn't try to cover up. Instead, she carefully scanned the living room and hallway leading back to her bedroom and bathroom. The apartment was empty.

She took three steps back toward the hallway and scooped up her towel, wrapping it around her while she tried to keep her eyes on the hallway back to her bedroom. That had to be where the intruder had hidden, probably to catch her unaware when she left the bathroom to get dressed.

But why move the egg?

"Look, I don't know who you are, but you're about to find out you snuck into the wrong girl's apartment. I suggest you announce yourself and come out with your hands up."

Nothing.

Quinn waited for almost a minute, listening to the silent apartment for any sign of who was back there. She even engaged her scent tracking skill in an attempt to see if it was some kind of supernatural.

She detected only the presence of last night's thrown-out leftovers in the trash can behind her. Quinn wrinkled her nose. She really should have taken that out to the dumpster last night before she went to bed.

Shaking her head, Quinn was about to start back and take on whoever was hiding back there when a tiny scraping noise came from down the hall.

The dragon egg rolled out into the hallway from the open bathroom doorway. It wobbled a little as it turned toward her and rolled to a stop at her feet.

Quinn stared down at it for the longest time. Her eyes tracked back down the hallway to the bathroom door, then she returned her gaze to the ovoid at her feet. Someone could have given it a shove from the bathroom, but how had they gotten it to turn the corner like that?

Quinn crouched and stared down at the egg. She set her hand on it and said, "Was it you all along, little guy?"

The faintest tremor vibrated the shell in her hand as she scooped up the egg, pulling it toward her to hold against her chest. When it came in contact with the silver amulet around her neck, the quivers were stronger for several seconds.

That was definitely not her imagination that time. It really moved.

Aurora hadn't said anything about the egg moving on its own when she'd had to let Quinn take it home with her. It seemed like a big thing to omit from the care instructions for a dragon egg. All the Fae princess had said at the time was to hold onto it and keep it safe until the year was up, and it was available to imprint on someone else again.

Quinn started back toward her bedroom, leading with her knife because she still half-expected to discover the missing intruder. There was no one in her room, though.

Setting the egg back down on her bed, Quinn finished toweling off and got dressed to go to sleep.

As she pulled on the oversized T-shirt, she yawned and said, "I'm so tired. I hope Clark turns up something to do in the city besides constantly training. I don't think I can take much more of what that woman is doing to me." Quinn sat down next to the polished green shell and laid her hand on it. It quivered.

"You're lucky. You don't have a mother hovering over you all the time. It's like she's trying to make up for lost time in a single week."

Another vibration, a double one this time.

Quinn glanced at the shiny surface of the shell, peering at it as if she could picture the tiny dragon inside. Could it really hear her?

"Look, I know I should be grateful Naomi is around. It is better than when I thought she was dead for all those years. Is that what you want me to say?"

A single humming buzz came through the shell.

"Fine. I'm glad she's here. There, I said it, so I hope you're happy. But don't expect me to tell Naomi that. I'm still mad at her."

Buzz, buzz.

"I don't care what you think. You aren't supposed to know who your mother is. You were laid a hundred and fifty years ago."

There was nothing for a few seconds, then the egg vibrated very softly for a long time before going still.

Quinn suddenly felt awful. She'd just teased a baby dragon about being an orphan just like she'd been.

Her eyes teared up, and she lay down beside it and pulled it close, stroking the smooth shell while she whispered, "I'm sorry" over and over.

She fell asleep a few minutes later, hugging her new friend.

CHAPTER FIVE

Quinn woke to a buzzing vibration the next morning.

"Hey," she muttered, struggling to wake up. She stroked the egg still cradled in her arms. "I said I was sorry."

The buzzing sounded again, and she realized it wasn't coming from the egg. Lifting her head, she looked around and saw her phone lit up on the nightstand. When she saw the time, 9:14 AM, she groaned.

She reached out and picked it up. It was Clark, and she sat up and tapped the screen to answer as she rubbed the sleep from her eyes with her other hand.

"Uh, yeah. I was just coming down for training. I overslept."

"Forget about that. I just got back after being out on a stakeout all night. Something's up. Meet me down in the bar. I'm getting breakfast."

"I'll be right there." Quinn stood up and glanced in the

mirror over the beat-up old dresser. "Um, give me ten, maybe fifteen minutes."

Clark hung up instead of responding. Quinn took that as tacit approval of her timeline. She'd fallen asleep without brushing her wet hair, and now it was a mess. She needed another shower to get it straightened out.

She picked up the towel from where it had hung over a chair to dry overnight. The egg was on the bed just below her pillow. She patted it and said, "You stay here this time. I've got to move fast, okay?"

It vibrated long and slow beneath her fingertips. She smiled and headed for the bathroom.

It was closer to twenty minutes by the time she got downstairs. She was still brushing her hair and pulling it back into a damp ponytail as she entered the bar.

The only occupied table in the place held Clark and Naomi. They sat hunched over, talking earnestly about something.

"Hey," Quinn said, noticing Clark's bowl of cold cereal and glancing around. "Is Juni or one of the other waitresses here.? I'd like to order some breakfast."

"Just grab some Toasty Oats from behind the bar like I did. There's a carton of milk in the cold case with the beer."

Naomi looked up as Quinn started toward the bar to grab some cereal. "I hope you got some sleep, kiddo. I know I've been riding you pretty hard. I figured you'd earned a little extra time."

Quinn crouched behind the bar and grabbed the box of cereal, then popped back up. "Uh, yeah, thank you, I guess. I was tired when I finally got to bed last night."

Naomi nodded and turned back to Clark. The two of

them went back to whatever deep conversation was occupying them. Quinn couldn't pick up what they were talking about all the way over at the bar.

Sliding open the lid to the cold case behind the bar, she leaned in and grabbed a half-gallon of milk from amidst the various bottles of beer. She looked around for where Clark had gotten the bowl and then shrugged and snagged an empty beer mug from a shelf beside the sink.

Quinn filled the mug with the puffed rings of cereal and poured milk over it until it was half-full. Putting the box and the carton away, she grabbed a long-handled cocktail spoon from top of the bar and returned to the table to sit and eat.

It was awkward getting both milk and cereal in a single spoonful, and soon she gave up. Instead, she spooned up some of the circular rings, and after she popped them in her mouth, tilted the mug to get milk, too. It worked well enough, and she smiled.

Quinn glanced up and saw Naomi watching her with a big grin as she ate.

"What? Did I do something wrong?"

"No," Naomi replied. Her grin broadened. "Not a thing."

Not sure what to make of the woman's response, Quinn scooped up another spoonful of cereal and turned to Clark. "So, what's up? You said you found something."

"Remember when I said there had been mysterious disappearances I needed to look into?"

"Yeah," Quinn said. "Did you track it back to some of Handon's goons still hanging around after we got rid of him?"

"I suspected that at first since they were the last group

like that to operate openly in the city. There's no connection to Handon that I can find, though. I'm going to have Taylor kick in some of her tech witch skills to see if she can locate any connection, but my gut tells me there isn't."

Quinn shrugged and looked from Clark to Naomi and back again. "Okay, then what is it? A new gang moving in to fill the void?"

Naomi said, "That's a good thought, but I think the best clue is in the people who've gone missing. They're shifters."

"So, somebody is kidnapping werewolves?" Quinn asked. "Do we need to warn Taylor?"

"They're not werewolves," Clark said. "They're badger-folk."

Quinn laughed, "A freaking werebadger? That's a thing?"

Naomi chuckled. "They're rare, but yeah, they're a thing, as you put it." Turning to Clark, she said, "I didn't know there was a colony here in Baltimore."

He nodded. "They came here looking for work years ago when the mines in West Virginia cut back production. There isn't much excavation work here, but they've adapted to working for local contractors operating digging equipment for foundations and such."

"Why would anyone attack them specifically?" Quinn asked. "Are any other shifter groups being targeted?"

"Not that I can see," Clark replied. "I've asked around, and everything else seems stable in the city right now."

Quinn crunched through another mouthful of cereal and chased it with a gulp of milk. "So, do we need to check this out? I'm ready to be on the street again. I don't know about Naomi, but I'm getting a little stir-crazy, staying in here all the time."

Clark smiled. "Is it because your moth…I mean, Naomi is running you ragged?"

"I can handle it," Quinn said. She glanced at Naomi, who smiled at her. Quinn sat up straighter. "I thought you might want some help. That's all."

"I want to check with Taylor and Miranda. If they have the VR system back up and running, it might be a good test for it and the new skills they want you to try out."

The changes Taylor had hinted at the last time they talked excited Quinn. The tech witch hadn't been very forthcoming, and she'd changed the subject when Quinn pressed her on it. She guessed she'd find out what they were soon enough.

"I'd love to get back into the system again. Naomi hasn't had a chance to see what I can do except for the big fight with Handon. We were all too distracted to take in everything properly then."

"It would be nice to see how the virtual reality stuff works," the vampire said. "Handon didn't talk much about that side of his operation with me."

Quinn clapped her hands together. "Good, it's settled. I'll go find Taylor and see where she and Miranda are on getting the new system up and running."

She got up and turned to leave.

Clark raised a hand to stop her, pointing to the empty mug on the table. "Clear that for Juni. Let's be respectful and not create extra work for her when we're down here after hours."

Quinn nodded and took the mug back to the bar. She leaned over the top and set it down in the stainless-steel sink. She stood up and turned just in time to see Taylor and Miranda come out from the club's back door that led to the storerooms and underground tunnels.

Taylor's big grin as she approached Clark and Naomi at the table got Quinn excited again. Things must be going well for Taylor to look so happy.

The tech witch stopped at the table. No, that wasn't right. It was more like she bounced beside the table, looking back and forth from Clark to Naomi.

Quinn walked up and realized from Clark's amused grin that he was enjoying watching Taylor wait for someone to ask her why she was so energized. The girl looked like she was about to burst.

Naomi glanced at Clark and said, "I suppose one of us should ask her what she has to say?"

"That would be best, I guess. Do you want to do the honors?"

Naomi shook her head. "I'm the newest member here. I think it should be you."

Quinn laughed. "Oh, come on, you two. Don't torture her. Taylor, what did you want to announce?"

"I finished, and it's better than I'd hoped. Miranda had ideas on adjusting the VirSync interface we acquired to take into account things we learned while building our own. We guessed on some stuff for the cobbled-together system we created. It turns out we invented new tech that enhances their professional system."

"It was Taylor who did all the hard work," Miranda said,

hovering beside the tech witch. "I just made some suggestions. She had to go through the trial and error process to make it all function."

Clark smiled. "What did you do, add a turbocharger to it?"

"Close," Taylor said, then the words started tumbling out. "We got the idea from the spells and rituals listed in the *Life Tome*. We figured the VR interface was the perfect place to add some additional functionality, and we had all those magical abilities just sitting there ready to be used. It took a lot of experimentation, and we've both been working almost non-stop for two days, but we finally got the first two of them to function."

"We think," Miranda countered. "We won't know for sure until Quinn gets in there and tries it. Only then will we know for sure if what we tried to do works."

Naomi leaned forward. "What sort of spells and rituals? Some of those things are for special occasions and require years of training to carry out safely."

Taylor waved a hand in the air. "Nothing too crazy. We found a way to give Quinn the ability to expand her stamina capacity. Think of it as a boost in her available life force."

"Okay, that's useful," Clark said. "It's also impressive. I never had much luck with spells to draw in life energy."

"Me neither," Naomi said. "What else?"

"Spells," Taylor and Miranda said together.

"You already said that," Clark said. "What kind of spells?"

"Just about anything, really," Taylor said. "Simple stuff

at first. But depending on how much Quinn can see once she gets in there, it could be quite significant as she levels up. To start with, it'll be focused on her ability to sense, and in a limited way, read magical energy used by someone else."

Quinn remembered some of the simple spells she'd seen Clark use, like unlocking doors with the wave of his hand. That would be useful.

Miranda said, "It'll start with Quinn learning to see the magical spectrum and the energy flows around her in the natural world. Once she can do that, we can try to teach her to see others who use magic. Eventually, she should be able to learn specific spells."

"When can I get in there and see?" Quinn asked. "Clark has a mission for us."

Taylor smiled. "It's ready now."

Miranda interrupted her. "But we're going to wait until after Taylor gets some rest. She's been running on adrenaline and caffeine for two days now. She shouldn't be expending more energy. It could be dangerous for both of you."

Both Quinn's and Taylor's shoulders sagged. Then Quinn noticed the circles under her friend's eyes and a general weariness in the way she carried herself.

"Miranda's right, T." Quinn smiled, hoping she hid her disappointment. "You get some rest. I can wait until tomorrow or the next day, once you get your strength back."

"Quinn's right," Clark said. "It wouldn't do to burn out our resident tech witch. Go up to your apartment. We'll still be here when you get back."

Naomi added, "Miranda and I can work with Quinn in the meantime. There are some exercises I remember that are supposed to help attune a Hunter trainee to magical energy."

"They're probably very similar to what I learned in my coven when I was growing up," Miranda added. "Between the two of us, I think we can come up with something that will work."

Clark nodded. "Good, it's settled then. We'll put Quinn through the new exercises, and when you're all rested, we'll pop her back into the VR world and see what she can do."

Taylor looked at Quinn.

"Go, I'll be fine. I live for training, remember?"

Taylor smiled and turned toward the door leading to the apartments.

Quinn waited for her friend to leave before she said, "We can go out and check on those badger shifters while you teach me to see magic, right?"

Naomi smiled and said, "No, dear. Those exercises are not suited to the field. We'll be working here in the practice arena until Taylor is back up to strength."

Miranda nodded. "It's not that bad. Think of it as super-strenuous stationary yoga."

"I don't think I like the sound of that."

"Nonsense." Naomi grinned. "You just need to get into the groove with the routine. Come on. We'll get you dialed in in no time."

Quinn bit back her groan, disappointed she wasn't going to go into the VR system sooner. She understood the need to watch out for Taylor, though. In her own way, she was as competitive and focused as Quinn was.

Naomi stood to head to the training room and Quinn followed, with Miranda right behind her. Time to see if she could learn to see magic.

CHAPTER SIX

Quinn did learn what she needed to see the barest hints of magical energy before Taylor was ready. A day and a half of the so-called yoga exercises Miranda and Naomi devised for her exhausted her. It made her not so sure she wanted to learn to use magic on her own.

She said as much while the others prepped the VR system to send her inside after dinner on the second day.

"Don't worry," Naomi said as Quinn sat on the wooden table beside Taylor's equipment. "The hardest part is over. It takes a shock to the body for someone to break through to the magical realm."

Miranda nodded. "Being a Huntress got you halfway there. We had to bring you the rest of the way. The good news is, it worked. Now you'll know what to look for inside the VR system, at least once you unlock whatever you have to unlock in there."

Quinn turned to Taylor, surprised by Miranda's statement. "You don't know what I need to do, but this works inside the VR system?"

Taylor shrugged. "I can figure out how to add the spells to the code once it's wired into the system, but I still don't know exactly how you access the interface the way you do. You'll have to try it once you're inside. Maybe it'll just show up as a new button or whatever in the display you see."

Quinn didn't like how little Taylor knew about what she might be able to do, but she understood why her friend couldn't give her a better explanation. She didn't know how she'd stumbled upon half the stuff she could do either. At least, now she'd know what she saw when someone used magic once she unlocked the skill in VR, and it should translate across the interface to the real world. That would allow her to build on the skill and do more with it.

Taylor went back to her checklist as she prepped for the system to go live. Quinn tapped her earpiece. "Clark, how close are you to the rendezvous point? I'm ready to go in on this end."

"I should be there in five minutes. Go into the system, and I'll meet you outside the restaurant. Remember, Quinn, do not go inside by yourself. These people are extremely skittish. I need to introduce you before they'll accept you."

"Got it. I'll wait in the parking lot for you to get there. See you in a few."

Quinn nodded to Taylor and the two other women as she lay back and put on the VR headset and goggles. "Ready when you are, T."

The system started to hum with a smooth tone, unlike the way their older, makeshift system had whined as the power ramped up. Taylor used the appropriated VirSync proprietary gear now. Quinn hoped the transition to and from VR was smoother. She was about to find out.

The faint light from the room that passed through the goggles faded to darkness. The sensation of falling backward took over as it all went black and she dove into VR once again.

Quinn woke seconds later, ready to double over retching like she usually did. That didn't happen, though. She smiled.

Tapping her earpiece, Quinn said, "No hurling this time, T. Good work."

"We aim to please. I just checked the GPS tracker on Clark's phone. He's still a few minutes away."

"That's all right. I'll wait for him out here."

Quinn checked the area to get her bearings. She was supposed to have materialized in the back corner of a parking lot behind the restaurant owned by the leader of this small shifter community. The place was supposed to be run by the one Clark used as his point of contact.

Quinn dipped a hand into her pocket to check her phone while she waited. Her hand stopped halfway there when a disturbance over by the restaurant caught her attention.

An ear-wrenching snarl pierced the night, followed by a woman's laugh. Quinn didn't like the sound of that snarl, although it didn't seem like the other voice was scared. Maybe it was nervous, hysterical laughter? Clark had said to hang back, but if someone was being attacked, she should intervene, right?

The snarl had lowered in volume, but Quinn still picked up a persistent low, constant growl as she started across the lot. She approached and ducked behind a car, muttering "mist" to herself. Quinn's form blended into the night's shadows. It was best to stay out of sight for the time being, at least until she knew what was going on.

Slipping out from behind the car, she moved closer until she spotted a tall redheaded woman standing with her back to Quinn. She wore a red and black leather head-to-toe suit. The strange superhero costume looked like it had padding or maybe body armor at key locations. Even with the armor, the suit accentuated the woman's smooth curves. Quinn instantly envied this other woman, if only for the cool outfit.

Opposite the redhead stood a fur-covered humanoid creature about four and a half feet tall, wearing what looked like a dress and an apron. A white and black stripe ran from her forehead all the way down her back, at least as far as Quinn could see when the creature twisted her head to look around. She had to be a werebadger.

The shifter hopped from foot to foot with agitation. She held her clawed hands rigid at chest height, ready to fight or defend herself.

"You can get wound up all you want," the taller woman said in a crisp upper-class British accent. "You know the mistress is not going to let you go back on your agreement. That's the only way your particular family problem gets solved. Do you understand? I don't want to come back here and have to tell you again."

The werebadger's snarl increased in volume for an instant, and Quinn was sure she was going to attack.

The woman thought so, too. She brought her right hand into view, holding a samurai sword so its tip hovered a few inches from the shifter's throat. The threat was clear.

Quinn still couldn't see her face, and she wondered who this woman was. She wanted to recognize her if they ran into each other again.

Checking the parking lot entrance for Clark, Quinn ran through her options as she tried to decide what to do. He should be here at any moment, but maybe she should intervene.

She reached for her Bowie, in the sheath beneath her right arm, but she never got to it.

The woman in red raised her left hand and snapped her fingers, disappearing from view in a single instant.

One minute she was standing there, and the next, she was gone.

Quinn looked in all directions for the woman, but there was no sign of her. It was like she had teleported away. Or maybe she was using a VR system like Quinn's?

On a whim, she ran through a quick exercise from her training with Naomi and Miranda. Quinn focused on the area where the woman had stood and caught the trailing edge of two glowing ribbons of magic leading across the lot and around the restaurant building.

The woman was gone, but Quinn now knew she'd used some sort of magic concealment spell to hide as she left.

The werebadger had been as startled as Quinn was by the woman's sudden disappearance. The shifter also looked around the lot for a few seconds, then changed back into human form. An older gray-haired woman wearing a pale blue dress and a kitchen apron now stood in the center of the lot. She smoothed the apron she wore over her dress before heading to the restaurant's kitchen entrance.

Quinn continued her search of the magical spectrum for the redhead, just to be sure she hadn't circled around to attack her from behind. All the residual magic of her passing had faded and there were no other visible signs, at least not that Quinn could make out. She let go of the slight trance she'd used to see the flows. As soon as she did, a new icon popped up in her HUD. She concentrated on it, and a description called it *Arcane Sight*.

Well, that answered that question. At least she now knew how to find that particular skill again in a hurry.

Clark's beat-up sedan turned into the parking lot about a minute later. He drove to the rear and pulled into a spot near the back corner.

After a last check for the woman in red, Quinn shook her head and headed back to meet him. She wasn't sure what she had just witnessed, but she knew he'd want to know about it before he went inside to confront the were-badger clan or pack or whatever it was called. If that whole confrontation had been about the disappearances, they knew a lot more about what had happened to their lost people than they'd told Clark.

Quinn canceled her shadow-hiding as she approached Clark's car.

He got out and spotted her walking his way. "I thought I told you to wait until I got here?."

"I was going to, but something happened that needed

investigation." Quinn went on to tell Clark about the strange exchange between the intruder and the old werebadger woman.

"That sounds like you saw Inez, the matriarch of this den. She owns the restaurant."

"Who was the other woman, though?"

Clark shook his head. "No clue. You sure about what you overheard?"

"Yep. I couldn't tell if she was in on the disappearances or helping to find the missing people. She did draw her sword on the old shifter, though. That's not usually the act of someone offering to help."

"Maybe," Clark said. "You said Inez was growling. Werebadgers are prickly at the best of times. It doesn't take much for them to get angry, even at people they know. I need to get in there and talk to her to see what happened."

Clark gestured for Quinn to follow him as he started toward the restaurant. "Be quiet in there and let me do the talking. Inez knows me. All you have to do is stand behind me. Oh, and try to smile and project calm."

"You act like I can't do that," Quinn shot back.

"Just do what I say and don't react to anything."

Quinn started to reply, but Clark's sharp glance stopped her. They'd almost reached the kitchen entrance, and it was probably not a good idea to be arguing as they went inside.

Clark stood at the screen door, with Quinn right behind him. He rapped on the frame and waited. The first thing she noticed as she looked inside at what she could see of the kitchen area was how short everyone who darted past the doorway was. All of them were around five feet tall, and a few were shorter than Inez. Quinn couldn't see the cooking area from here, so she only saw three or four who went to and from what looked like a pantry. From the sound of the rest of the kitchen around the corner, the place was bustling. It smelled delicious.

Inez came to the door just as Clark was about to knock again. She spotted him and Quinn and frowned, wiping her hands on a towel hanging from her apron before walking their way. From the way she pressed her lips together into a thin line, Quinn guessed she wasn't happy to see them. Odd that she didn't seem scared of them the way she'd been with the sword-wielding redhead. She stood inside the door without inviting them in.

"Hello, Inez," Clark said through the screen door. "I told you I'd come back with my assistant to see what we could do to help you."

"And I told you I didn't need it."

"We both know that's not true. You've never turned down help from the Hunters before. I remember my father talking about you."

"Your father is long dead, and the Hunters are no more. We must all fend for ourselves as best we can."

Quinn tamped down the heat rising within her. Who was this woman to talk to Clark like that when he was here to help?

Clark must've sensed her tension because he dropped his hand to his side, palm facing Quinn.

The instruction was clear, and she tried to take a deep breath and let it out slowly without the old woman noticing.

"It is true the old Hunter clans are no longer here, but Quinn and I have worked hard to take on that role in this community. You know what we did with John Handon and his followers. We can work to help you, too, if you'll let us."

Inez shook her head. "I no longer need your assistance. I should have called you to let you know. Now, I am busy with many customers tonight. I must get back to work."

Quinn glowered at Inez past Clark. This woman wasn't going to push them away when she knew the lady was lying. "What about your redheaded visitor earlier? Is she helping you now, so you don't need us anymore?"

Clark shot Quinn an angry glare.

Inez's eyes darkened, and her brows lowered. "So, you've been spying on me and mine, Clark Hunter? You know how I feel about deception."

"My associate arrived before me and witnessed the encounter you had earlier. That is all. I have not been back since I left here a few nights ago."

Inez considered what he had said and answered with a brief nod. Quinn couldn't tell if it was agreement or acknowledgment.

"I saw her threatening you," Quinn said. "Tell us what is going on. We can protect you."

Inez turned her deep-brown eyes on Quinn, boring them into her like a drill. "Foolish girl, you do not know what you're talking about. What you think you saw is incorrect. That woman is a business contact with whom I have made a specific arrangement. It is none of your concern."

She turned back to Clark and continued, "I have asked you to leave nicely. Don't make me resort to force."

Inez clapped twice quickly, and four members of the kitchen staff came around the corner and stood behind her. Each held a knife or another weapon, and a low, buzzing snarl filled the air.

The hairs on the back of Quinn's neck rose up in reaction to the sound. Without thinking, she blurted, "We're not scared of you. We—"

Clark raised his arm and pushed Quinn back to stand behind him and to the side. "What she means to say is we were just leaving. I don't know what kind of game you're playing here, Inez. We both know you need my help, but I'll respect your wishes for the time being. You know where to find me if you want to reach out. Until then, I'll keep my distance and let you tend to your affairs by yourself."

Inez held Clark's steady gaze for a few seconds and then nodded. She clapped once, and the kitchen activity resumed as if nothing had happened. Quinn detected an air of desperate readiness, and she wondered if it had been there all along.

Clark nodded to her, and Quinn took the hint. She walked across the parking lot, with Clark just behind her. They were both silent.

"What the heck, Clark?" Quinn said when she reached the rear of Clark's sedan. "You know she was lying, and you let her back you down like she was your master."

"You know anything about badgers, Quinn?"

She shook her head. She'd seen a video once online, but it was an animal fighting a snake or something. She didn't remember specifics.

"They're among the most tenacious and fierce animals

there are. I'd say pound for pound, they're the most dangerous mammals on the planet when backed into a corner. The human shifter version is no different, and you'll get nowhere but hurt trying to bully them."

"But that other woman with the sword threatened Inez, and she backed down without a second thought."

"Exactly," Clark said. He paused and waited as if he expected an answer.

Pondering what he'd just said and what she'd seen, Quinn considered, then said, "If Inez is scared of the redhead, we should be, too. Is that it?"

"'Scared' might not be the right word, but 'cautious' certainly is. Whoever she is or represents, this newcomer is worth handling with care until we know more. Somehow, someone has found a way to hold something over Inez's head, forcing her to go along with whatever's happening."

"So, what now?"

"Now we go home. You resume your training while I figure out another way to help Inez without her knowing it. That'll have to do until we can get a handle on what's going on."

Clark got in his car and fired up the engine. Quinn stood by the driver's door as he wound the window down.

"I'll catch you back at O'Malley's. We can sit down there, get some food, and talk to the others about everything. Maybe they'll have some insight on what to do next."

Clark backed out of his spot and headed for the street, leaving Quinn alone at the back of the parking lot. Returning to the corner near where she first arrived, Quinn tapped her earpiece and said, "T, you there? I'm ready to come back."

"Did you find out anything? How about new skills?"

"I'll tell you when I get back. Clark is on his way, too."

"Sounds good. Entering the return signal into the system now."

Quinn felt something tugging at her mind, and she closed her eyes as she fell into the blackness.

CHAPTER SEVEN

The whole clan except for Miranda sat in O'Malley's bar watching country-western line dancers do their thing while the honkytonk band played a song about a lost girl and a pickup truck. Or maybe it was about a lost pickup truck and a girl. Quinn could never be sure with those songs. She much preferred driving rock with girl-power angst behind it.

For the past hour and a half, ever since Clark had returned, the four of them had gone over the encounters at the werebadger restaurant across town. They'd gotten no closer to finding out what it all meant. Quinn wanted to return in secret and do some investigating.

She suggested it to Clark. "I know you want to respect Inez's wishes and her position, but if she's in trouble, maybe we have to act on her behalf until she can do it for herself."

"You can't sneak in there, Quinn. If they caught you, even if you survived their reaction, it might still unravel the trust I've sought to build over the years with them."

"I can take care of myself," she stated.

Naomi shook her head. "Clark's right. You don't get a second chance to build trust with werebadgers. Once you lose their confidence, it's gone forever. We need to be very careful about how we approach this."

"All right," Quinn said. "What's your solution?"

"I'm not sure," Naomi replied. "Clark, how did you originally discover some of them had gone missing? Did Inez reach out to you?"

"Oh, she'd never do that," Clark said. "She's far too proud to ask for help. No, I learned about it when I ran into Dameon Cool, the werewolf pack leader. He reached out to ask how Taylor was doing with her wolf side. He made an offhand comment about it, and I asked him for more info. He'd learned about it from a member of his pack. He offered to help her, too. Inez brushed him off, just like she did us."

Taylor said, "I say we send Quinn back in. If not into the restaurant, then maybe nearby so she can keep an eye on things. If she can track that redhead by her magical trail, she could follow her. She might lead us to where the missing people are."

Clark shook his head. "We're still not sure this newcomer is even part of the problem. She could be part of something else."

"Then we're back to where we started," Quinn said. Frustrated, she leaned back in her chair and looked around for Juni. She needed another soda.

That was when she saw the woman. She was the most beautiful girl she'd ever seen. She stood across the club in the dimly lit area near the entrance. She seemed to be about Quinn's age, with her hair pulled back in a ponytail. It looked light brown in the dim light, but Quinn wasn't sure. The woman wore tight blue jeans with knee-high black boots and a silky yellow blouse. A bright red leather jacket that came down to her waist topped it all off.

She moved with smooth grace when she walked farther into the bar. Quinn had often tried to pull off that walk, but she always felt like she didn't quite get it right. The girl stirred feelings she hadn't let herself experience for quite some time.

It took her several seconds to realize the woman wasn't alone. A dark-haired woman in her forties accompanied her. The other woman was dressed in a short, provocative black skirt and white button-down blouse, topped with a long black overcoat.

"I don't believe it," Naomi said in her seat beside Quinn. "It can't be!"

"What?" Clark asked, looking around. He stopped scanning the room when he reached the two women by the door. "Wait, is that…"

The dark-haired woman's eyes had been searching the crowded bar, and when they reached Quinn's group seated on the opposite side of the room, she smiled, tugged at the younger one's sleeve, and started their way.

As the pair got closer and walked through better-lit areas of the bar, Quinn realized the younger one's hair was dark auburn, not brown. Her feeling of attraction shifted to a sense of warning. There was something familiar about her.

Naomi stood and smiled. "Gemma Beckingsly, I can't believe it. How is it you're still alive?"

"What?" The woman's British accent gave her next question a hint of arrogance. "You didn't believe you were the only one to live through the purges, did you?"

"I suppose not, but after so much time, it's strange to see you now."

Clark cleared his throat. "She's right, Gemma. After things settled down following the purges, I tried reaching out on all the channels and methods I knew of to try to find other survivors. Why didn't you respond?"

"I kept tabs on what you were up to, but I couldn't trust that others hadn't compromised those communication methods. After what happened, we couldn't trust anyone, could we? Besides, my mission was far too important for that kind of mistake."

"What brings you here now?" Naomi asked. "You never do anything unless there's something in it for you."

"Well, as I said, I've been following what you've all been doing here, and I decided it was time to come out of hiding. I have to keep you from making a horrible mistake."

"What kind of mistake?" Clark asked.

"With her," Gemma replied, pointing at Quinn. "You see, I found the real Huntress, the one from the prophecy. I've been training her since right after the purges, making sure she learned all the lore and skills before they were lost to the ages."

Quinn stared at Gemma and said, "I'm sorry, what? You have your own Huntress?"

"Oh, I'm sorry, my dear. Where are my manners? Naomi, Clark, and uh, the rest of you, meet the real Huntress, Avery Skelton-Smythe."

The younger woman smiled at them each in turn,

including a big grin when she reached Quinn. "Hello, it's a pleasure to meet you all. Gemma has told me a great deal about everything you've been up to, preparing for my return."

Quinn's jaw dropped. That voice, the red hair. It all clicked.

"Clark, it's her. She's the one from the restaurant earlier. She was the one who threatened Inez."

Quinn drew her Bowie and stood, knocking her chair over backward. She readied herself for a fight, sure the other girl would pull a knife or maybe draw that samurai sword from out of thin air like she did earlier.

Everyone stared at her, her friends shocked by her response and accusation. Gemma's and Avery's confident smiles never changed, though. It was as if they'd expected Quinn's reaction.

Avery glanced at Gemma. "I told you I sensed someone else when I was talking with the old woman."

"So you did, my dear. You'd think I'd have learned by now to trust your excellent instincts." Gemma turned to Quinn. "If that was you, it seems that Clark has managed to teach you a few tricks in the short time since he discovered you. That will be very helpful. Avery needs competent followers to help her fulfill her destiny in the coming months."

Quinn put her hands on her hips and cocked her head to one side, staring at Avery, sizing her up. "I think there's been a mistake. I'm the Huntress; that's *my* thing. I came up with it."

Gemma laughed and looked at Clark and Naomi. "You've never told her of the prophecy, either of you?"

"I don't need them to tell me anything. I heard it myself. I got it directly from the hallowed dead clan leaders. They spoke to me." Quinn shifted her gaze to Avery again. "Has anyone spoken to you?"

The other girl hadn't moved or shown any emotion since Quinn had stood and drawn her weapon. It infuriated her.

After a few seconds of what looked like confusion in her eyes, Avery smiled, seeming to regain confidence. "When you've been raised to be something from birth, you don't need ghosts propping up your fantasies. My coming was foretold."

Quinn took a step toward Avery and Taylor jumped up and inserted herself between them, placing her hand on her best friend's chest. Avery still hadn't moved.

"Quinn, I think maybe we got off on the wrong foot with our guests here." Taylor turned to flag down Juni, who stood watching the confrontation from beside the next table. "Can you get two more chairs for us and some snacks. Maybe we can straighten this out over food."

Taylor turned back to Quinn and pressed her hand more firmly against her friend's chest until Quinn sat back down. Juni and another waitress arrived with two chairs and set them so Gemma and Avery could sit.

Gemma sat first and then gestured at the chair beside her without looking at Avery. The other Huntress sat down and crossed her legs.

Juni came over with her pad and pen out. "What can I get you two to drink?"

Gemma said, "This is a leprechaun bar, right?" She rolled her eyes when Juni nodded. "The wine is probably horrendous. I'll just have the best lager you have on tap. Avery here will have bottled mineral water.

That brought a smile to Quinn's lips. It looked like Gemma didn't let her protege have much fun. At least Quinn could order for herself, as long as she didn't order alcohol.

She'd tried it once right after they moved in. Juni had looked her over and shaken her head. "Sorry, hon, you've got to have a few more birthdays under your belt before I serve you. How about soda?"

Quinn blushed with embarrassment at the awkward memory. She glanced up and caught Avery staring at her with a wry grin on her face. Had she seen Quinn blush? Cursing under her breath, she looked away. That was just what she needed right now. She'd thought she was done with the popular-girl politics crap when she left high school.

Naomi cleared her throat after an awkward pause as Juni left to get the drinks and snacks. "What brings you here to America? I would have thought someone like you'd be living it up amidst the uber-rich in Europe. That's what the Gemma I used to know would be doing."

Quinn caught how Naomi was trying to mean-girl Gemma back. It seemed like she was doing it to help her daughter. It might have been endearing from a normal mother, but in this case, it only annoyed Quinn. She didn't need rescuing.

She began to say something when Avery leaned forward, staring hard at Naomi. "Gemma, she's a vampire." She sniffed and turned, her eyes widening as she looked at Taylor. "That one's a werewolf."

Naomi seemed startled, but it passed in a flash. She leaned back in her chair and smiled, letting her canines show.

Gemma's eyebrows shot up, and she looked around at the others at the table as if trying to see if any of the others were surprised by the revelations. When no one else reacted, she nodded and gave a toothy grin of her own.

"A vampire and a werewolf in addition to this orphan girl in your little rag-tag band, Clarkie? You really are slumming."

If her barb struck home, Clark didn't miss a beat. He lifted his beer and smiled as he sipped from it. "We have a ghost sorceress somewhere nearby, too, if you decide to stick around." He set his mug down. "Which brings us to why you're here, and what you and your girl here have to do with the disappearances in the south end of the city."

Gemma shook her head. "The incident earlier tonight is a little side job I'm commissioning. The werebadgers have the skills I need for something, and I want to hire them. That's all. I don't know anything about any disappearances. I only just now got into town. I told you when I walked in, the reason I'm here is your girl there."

Gemma pointed at Quinn and continued, "Word has started to spread in certain circles about the new Huntress in Baltimore. I've worked too hard training and raising Avery in secret, preparing her for her destiny. I'm not going to let your little experiment here expose the prophecy to the wrong people before it's time for her to fulfill it."

Naomi asked, "What if you're wrong, Gemma?"

"Wrong about what? The prophecy?"

"No, I believe in the prophecy. I've seen too much to discount it. No, I mean, what if you've bet on the wrong horse?"

"You think your little half-trained girl here is the one spoken of in legends and not Avery?" Gemma laughed. "I did my research before I came. She's been training for less than a year. You think she's able to compete with my Avery, who's been working for this all her life?"

Gemma shook her head, dismissing the question. She picked up her beer but stopped before she took a drink. "Wait, you're serious. You think you're right. Darling, I know you've somehow betrayed your oaths and become one of the undead. I can't believe you've fallen so far that you don't realize the difference between one raised in the right way with all the advantages and a wayward girl from the streets."

Naomi frowned and said, "You know, Gemma, when I first met you at boarding school after my parents moved to Europe, you were a prissy, stuck-up pain in the ass. You only tolerated me because of my father's position as the clan's ambassador. He and my mother told me I had to be diplomatic with you and the others, but I always wanted to show you what I really thought of you."

"What do you propose, my dear?" Gemma asked.

"Why don't we let the girls train together for a bit? That way, we can see who's the best. I'm sure one of them will outdo the other. Then we'll know which is the Huntress from all the tales."

Gemma smiled and nodded. "Done. It'll be a pleasure to take you down a peg again."

Quinn didn't know what to say. They all acted like she

wasn't sitting here. The only bright spot in this whole mess was that Avery's face displayed as much shock as hers.

Clark seemed as pleased by all this as Naomi was. That was typical. From his perspective, this was another chance to test Quinn. This time she'd go up against someone who had similar training.

Only Taylor seemed worried. When she caught Quinn looking her way, she forced a supportive smile onto her face and nodded. At least Taylor had her back.

Clark said, "It's settled, then. We can start tomorrow. In the meantime, have you been in town long? We have room here for you if you'd like a place to stay."

"I'm staying down near the harbor, but perhaps it would be good for Avery to stay close to the clan's chambers, now that you have taken them back. Could she perhaps bunk with your girl?"

"Hey!" Quinn and Avery said in unison.

Naomi laughed at the dual reaction. Quinn glared at her mother. She hoped Naomi would get the message. There was no way she'd allow this.

Naomi smiled and said, "I think that's a great idea. They can get to know each other's strengths and weaknesses up close and personal, the way we did back in our school days."

"Don't think young Quinn will gain any advantage from anything Avery can do. It would take her years to learn what Avery has."

"I wouldn't be so sure. Quinn has her own unique abilities."

Clark smiled. "It's settled, then. Avery can stay with

Quinn, and we'll begin the contest in the morning." He rubbed his hands together. "I can't wait."

Gemma nodded and stood. "Come, Avery, we will go and gather your things from the house, and I'll bring you back here so you can get started with your next test. I'll expect you to excel as you always do."

Avery stood. "Yes, ma'am."

From the steely look in her eyes, the other girl didn't want to go along with the plan any more than Quinn did. She didn't argue, though. She followed the older woman out through the bar's entrance.

Quinn watched the alleged Huntress leave. Despite the tension, she couldn't help enjoying the smooth grace of her walk and how she carried herself. Once she was sure they were gone, she turned back to Naomi and Clark. "What the heck? Am I some sort of racehorse for you to wager on now?"

Naomi ignored her. "That felt so good. How about you, Clark?"

"Oh, it did indeed. I met her on an exchange summer a few years before the purge. She toyed with all the boys in the clan, acting high and mighty because she was from what she called 'the real Hunter clans' back in the old country. I can't wait for Quinn to show her girl what for."

"Um, excuse me? I'm right here. You don't have to talk about me like I'm not. Aren't you going to ask my opinion about all of this?"

"All you need to do is show that fake Huntress that you're the real deal," Clark said. "You can do that, right?"

"Of course I can," Quinn replied. Deep in her gut, she might even have believed it. Avery seemed so sure of herself, though, except for the part at the very end when she found out she had to stay with Quinn.

"Good," Naomi said. "Then it's settled. Go up and make up your couch or something. You have extra sheets and blankets, yes?"

Quinn nodded, and Naomi smiled. "Then get to it. She'll be back here before you know it, and it's already late. Clark and I will stay here and work on training tests and scenarios for the two of you."

The Huntress walked across the bar, weaving through the line dancers near the bandstand. As she pulled the door to the apartment shut behind her, blocking out the noise, she muttered, "What the heck just happened?"

CHAPTER EIGHT

Quinn tapped her phone five times before she finally silenced the alarm. After rolling onto her back, she rubbed her eyes and stared at the ceiling, trying to get her bearings.

The toilet flushed, and footsteps padded down the hall toward the living room. It took a few seconds for Quinn to remember who it was, and then she groaned.

It was that girl. She was staying here, in Quinn's apartment.

Someday she would find a way to repay Clark and Naomi for this. For now, though, she had to get moving. She didn't want to be late for this little training competition the others had planned.

Slipping into her jeans, Quinn stumbled out into the kitchen to start the coffee maker. She was no good until she was well into cup number two.

"Why aren't you dressed? We'll be late."

Quinn started the coffee maker and pulled open the fridge to get the cream. She looked over her shoulder.

Avery stood there, fully dressed, with a red nylon and canvas gym bag hanging from a strap over her shoulder.

With a snort of laughter, Quinn said. "What are they gonna do, start without us?"

"That's not the point," Avery said, confusion and a hint of curiosity in her tone. "A Huntress must be reliable and steadfast above all things."

"Wow, that Gemma chick sure did a number on you. Why didn't *she* just become the Huntress? She could've saved herself the trouble of raising and training you."

Avery laughed. "That shows how much you don't know. Gemma cannot be the Huntress. She was raised to be a mage in the clan. Only certain individuals are suitable for the Hunter path."

"Ah, that makes sense," Quinn replied. "You know what they say."

"No, what?"

"Those who can't do, teach." Quinn pulled her now-full mug out from under the single-serve spigot and dumped three spoonfuls of sugar in, followed by enough cream to turn the black liquid the color of light caramel.

"I assure you, Gemma has been an excellent teacher. She raised me so I could learn all the clan lore, even with all that was lost in the purges."

Quinn sipped from her mug and said, "Yeah, like what?"

Avery thought for a few seconds and then smiled. "She taught me to master all the basics of the five elements."

Quinn tried to hide her confusion as she attempted to tick off the five in her head. Clark had never talked about them. A vague memory of Miranda and Taylor talking about something to do with magic and elements tickled her mind. She figured earth, wind, fire? Oh, and water, too. And…what else?

"You don't know them, do you?" Avery asked and grinned. "Gemma was right. You know nothing. You're a pretender. Watch and learn."

Avery snapped her fingers, opening her hand palm up. A one-inch tongue of flame appeared above her hand, hovering in the air. She smiled as she stared at Quinn, then closed her hand and snuffed out the flame.

Quinn turned away and set her half-empty coffee mug in the sink. She realized she'd clenched her other fist and forced herself to relax. Why was she trying to compete with this girl? She knew who she was.

Turning back, she said, "Nice party trick. Not sure what good it'll do you in a real fight."

"If you stop stalling and get ready for our training contest today, perhaps I'll show you up close and personal."

Quinn wasn't sure if that was a threat, but she knew Avery was right about one thing—she *was* stalling. Gritting her teeth, Quinn walked past her unwanted houseguest and returned to her bedroom to finish getting dressed. No second cup of coffee today.

Five minutes later, the two women walked downstairs and into O'Malley's to find Clark, Gemma, and Naomi standing there. None of them looked pleased.

"You're late," Clark said.

Gemma nodded. "I hope you're not picking up bad habits from this one, Avery. I've worked very hard to instill the necessary discipline into you."

"It won't happen again. I will come down without her tomorrow."

Gemma nodded and turned to Clark. "Lead the way. The sooner we complete the testing, the sooner you can lend us a hand in helping Avery assume her role as the true Huntress."

Naomi nodded and glanced at Clark. "Let's do this."

Clark gestured for them to follow him and started for the passage to the Hunter Chambers. Quinn wondered where they were going. She hoped it was the training maze she'd been through already. That would give her an advantage.

Instead of continuing down the long hall toward the underground chambers, he stopped at the large storeroom they'd converted into a training and sparring area. Quinn tried to hide her disappointment. This wasn't going to give her any advantage.

"Let's start with basic combat," Clark said as he opened the door and switched on the light. "I assume Avery has had combat training?"

"She's trained with the best weapons masters in the old country. She's more than well-trained. There are those who've called her a master in her own right." Gemma pointed to the practice weapons on the rack across the room. "Avery, select your weapon."

Avery smiled and crossed to the rack, perusing the array of blunted weapons before choosing a wooden samurai sword similar to the one Quinn had seen her wield before. She ran through a few practice swings to test the weight and balance. Then she executed a complex series of acrobatic attack sequences. Each sent her spinning and twisting through the air as she made her way back across the practice mat toward the others. She finished on one knee with her blade extended in Quinn's direction.

Quinn took a step backward before regaining her composure. She'd become distracted by the smoothness and ease with which Avery moved. She embodied beauty and strength at the same time, something Quinn had envied since the other had shown up in the bar the night before.

Stepping back beside Clark, she realized everyone's eyes were on her. Did they want her to do that, too? Clark and Naomi knew she couldn't begin to demonstrate the same level of mastery. She was good in a fight, but mostly she acted on instinct. Her early martial arts training at the city rec center, she'd used for simple self-defense on the street. It helped her with the training Clark had put her through, but it wasn't anything like what Avery had displayed.

After an awkward pause, Quinn walked to the weapons rack and picked up the practice Bowie. She stepped back on the mat, moving to the center and waiting for Avery to join her.

Avery stepped forward and glanced at Quinn's knife. "That's your weapon of choice? This is going to be easier than I thought."

"It suits me," Quinn replied.

Avery snorted and assumed a guard stance.

Quinn glanced at her blade, realizing the knife's disadvantage against the other girl's sword. She usually trained to fight against unarmed supernatural creatures, only having to fend off fangs and claws. Assuming a stance similar to Avery's, Quinn nodded and prepared to defend herself.

Gemma barked, "Begin."

Avery darted forward to strike at Quinn, moving so fast her form blurred as Quinn tried to track and follow her. The only time Quinn had seen that kind of speed had been when watching Naomi move in combat. She'd always assumed her mother's speed had to do with her vampire strength. Now she realized it came at least in part from her early Hunter training.

The practice katana slashed in at her and almost connected. Quinn barely managed to shift her Bowie around and parry the attack. She didn't block the follow-up kick Avery launched.

It caught her in the shoulder. Quinn grunted as the spinning kick knocked her to the mat. She rolled to try to put some distance between herself and Avery.

Quinn came up on one knee, preparing to stand and stopped. Avery's wooden blade rested against her throat.

"Yield."

Quinn held her hands out at her side, letting her practice Bowie drop to the mat beside her. "I yield."

Avery pulled the blade away and moved back to the center of the mat.

Quinn picked up her blade and stood, shaking her head. She hadn't even had a chance to open her HUD and dial up stamina to boost her strength and speed. It had been over in a few seconds.

"Again," Clark said. He glared at Quinn. "You can do better than that."

Quinn nodded and walked back to the center of the

mat. This time she opened her HUD and drew twenty-five percent off her stamina bar, adding to her strength and speed. She wished she knew how young hunter trainees learned how to do this naturally.

"Begin," Gemma said.

This time Quinn was ready, and she met the incoming attack sequence without getting knocked down. She was unable to launch any attacks of her own, though. All her efforts focused on defense.

When Avery's initial attack didn't succeed in taking Quinn out, the other Huntress adjusted by using more complex attacks.

Clark had never moved like this in their training bouts, and Quinn struggled against combination attacks that had Avery backing her around the practice mat.

In desperation, Quinn launched a thrust at what she thought was an opening in Avery's formidable defenses. The other girl twisted aside, so it met only air. She moved so fast, it caught Quinn completely by surprise.

Avery chopped down, catching Quinn's forearm with the blunt edge of her blade.

Sharp pain stunned the muscles in Quinn's wrist and hand. Once again, her blade dropped to the mat.

"Again," Clark said, his dispassionate voice not matching the angry fire Quinn saw in his eyes.

Naomi's face showed pity for her daughter. That angered Quinn even more than the look on Clark's face.

Rubbing at her bruised forearm, Quinn tried to restore feeling to her tingling fingers. She bent down and retrieved her knife, returning to the center of the mat.

"Again," Clark repeated.

She knew Clark was going to keep her at this until she found a way to beat the other girl. Quinn resigned herself to a long morning. Brushing away the dark hairs that had escaped her ponytail to dangle at the side of her face, Quinn assumed a ready stance once again, drawing even more power from her stamina bar.

Gemma sounded almost amused as she said, "Begin."

Two hours later, Quinn stared at the mat from her hands and knees. Her stamina bar flashed red. She gasped to catch her breath and fight through the exhaustion.

Tilting her head, Quinn looked at Avery. She had rolled to her side and started to rise after Quinn's surprise snap forward kick had launched her across the mat. It was only the third time she'd taken down the other girl all morning.

Quinn stood, stretching her aching and bruised body as she did.

"Enough," Naomi said. "I think Gemma has made her point."

"So, you concede that Avery is the true Huntress of prophecy?" Gemma asked.

"No," Naomi said. "But you have demonstrated Avery has certain martial skills Quinn needs to improve upon."

"Oh, come now, my dear. How can you deny the obvious? Avery is more a Huntress than your girl will ever be. Admit it."

Clark stepped in and placed a hand on Naomi's shoulder. "I think all Quinn has proven is that she doesn't stay down long when she falls."

Gemma started to counter him, and Clark held up a hand to forestall her. "Let's let the ladies clean up and get something to drink up in Quinn's apartment while we go order us all lunch. They can join us after they've changed."

Quinn caught Clark's glance in her direction. She nodded a thank you. His facial expression showed his disappointment and little else. She walked over to the weapons rack to return the wooden Bowie to it.

Avery came up and replaced her sword in its position with the other practice weapons. She rubbed at her wrist and forearm. "A little heavier than my sword, but that's a good thing in a practice weapon, don't you think?"

Quinn couldn't understand how Avery could still be as fresh as she was. Even plastered with sweat from their sparring, she looked like she could keep going for another two hours.

"How do you do it?" Quinn asked.

"Do what?"

"Why are you not completely wiped out by what we just did? I know you won most of the bouts, but I got some good attacks in, and you don't seem to be nearly as exhausted as I am."

"I wondered about that, too," Avery said. "Why didn't you refresh yourself?"

"We didn't get a break until now."

"It's a way to tap into your core powers and rejuvenate your body during a conflict. You never learned to do that? It's one of the first things they teach a young initiate."

Quinn shook her head. "Clark must've forgotten that lesson, among other things."

Avery looked over her shoulder to be sure they were alone. The others had left. "I can try to show you later if you want."

Quinn's gut reaction was to snap a sharp no, but she surprised herself. "That would be nice if you think you can?"

Avery smiled. "It can't hurt to try. We can do it tonight after dinner."

Quinn nodded and returned the other girl's smile. The biggest pain about all this was that Avery wasn't a horrible person. Under other circumstances, she and Quinn might have become friends, or maybe even more, instead of being rivals.

"Come on," Quinn said. "Let's go up to the apartment and shower and change. Then we can go eat. I could use some food to recharge."

Avery nodded and followed her out of the sparring room.

CHAPTER NINE

By the end of the second day of training, Quinn was sure Clark was without a doubt the worst instructor in the world, followed closely by every other sensei she'd had growing up. Avery continued to beat back everything Quinn managed to throw at her while breaking through each of Quinn's carefully crafted defensive sequences.

The worst part wasn't that Quinn was losing. She'd lost before, and her competitive nature told her she'd find a way through it. There was no quit in her.

No, the worst of it was how likable Avery was, at least when she wasn't lording her "true Huntress" status over Quinn. Even then, it wasn't gloating. She acted like she was just stating a fact.

Avery's striking beauty and self-confidence attracted Quinn to her so much that, despite the beatings she took, she still wanted to be around the other Huntress. She wanted to keep trying to show they were at least equals in many ways.

There was also a naiveté in Avery that puzzled Quinn.

Despite being raised in Europe and having all that excellent training and skill under her belt, Avery hadn't lived much.

Quinn's time in the foster care system and on the streets had forced her to grow up fast. She had learned many skills early on, including the ability to read people and judge their intentions toward her, based on body language alone. Avery, on the other hand, seemed sheltered. Sure, she could kill a marauding werewolf without missing a beat, but she misread basic cues from Quinn about wanting her out of the apartment or when it was time to stop talking and go to bed.

After dinner on that second day, once they got upstairs, Quinn finally pressed the point. They entered the apartment after not saying a word to each other all through dinner and on the walk up from the bar afterward.

Despite Quinn's ignoring her for the last hour and a half, Avery acted like nothing was wrong. She put her gear down on the small table in the kitchenette and said, "Hey, do you want to shower first, or can I claim the honor since I won all the bouts today?"

"We should fight for it? Is that what you're saying?" Quinn snapped back.

Avery's jaw dropped, and she gaped at Quinn. "Are you angry with me?"

"Oh, for God's sake, cut the act. You can't be that stupid. You know so much about everything else in the world."

"Stupid about what?" Avery asked.

Judging from her confused expression, Quinn's estimate of Avery's ability to read social cues was right on target.

Quinn spread her arms and indicated the apartment as she turned in place. "About all this, about me, about what you're trying to do here. It's like you don't see what Gemma instigated by bringing you here."

"I don't understand. We came here to enlist your help in our mission to restore the clans through the prophecy of the Huntress. She told you that when we first arrived. I was there, remember?"

"That's what she told us, but you see, we already had our own clan here in Baltimore. We didn't need anyone coming in to try to show us what we were doing wrong."

"But— "

Quinn cut Avery off. "Never mind. You're not going to figure it out anytime soon. This is my apartment, so I'm taking the first shower. You can wait until I'm finished."

Avery didn't answer as Quinn went into her room, slamming the door. As it shut, she smiled, taking satisfaction with how clueless the European Huntress seemed about her outburst.

Good, Quinn thought. Avery could ponder it while she cleaned up and see how she liked feeling on the outside for a change.

Quinn went into her bedroom and stripped down, then headed into the bathroom to soak under the hot spray of the showerhead while she soothed her bruises from the last two days of defeats.

Twenty minutes later, Quinn returned to her room and changed into a pair of sweatpants from her high school lacrosse team. She also pulled on a black t-shirt with a stylized Maryland flag in the shape of a crab on it.

As she sat on her bed and brushed out her long dark

hair, Quinn listened to the shower running. Her thoughts drifted to Avery, who was probably trying to relax her own tired muscles. Quinn had landed more than a few blows today, although not as many as Avery had. Did the other girl have bruises on that pale, freckled skin?

Thinking of Avery in the shower distracted Quinn so much she didn't see the dragon egg. It was perched on her pillow, where it had been all day while she was away. It rocked back and forth a few times until it rolled free of the pillow and across the blanket to nudge Quinn's hip. She glanced down and snorted a laugh.

"What? Do you think I'm being too hard on her?"

The egg quivered once and rocked back and forth before settling back into stillness.

"That's easy for you to say. It's not like you have some already-hatched super-hot, dragon girl around telling how you're not measuring up."

A long vibration against her hip gave Quinn the impression the thing was chuckling at her.

"Okay, you can stop right there. I get it. She's attractive. Hell, she's hot, even. That doesn't mean I want anything to happen between us. It's not like we have anything in common at all."

The egg didn't move this time.

"Oh, no comment?" She shook her head. "What good is it to have a secret romance to share with someone if you're not going to respond when I drop a real question on you?"

"Who are you talking to?" Avery, wrapped in a towel, asked from the open door.

Quinn's head jerked around, and she felt the heat rising to her face. How much had she heard?

"Um, I didn't hear you come out of the shower."

"Gemma says I'm naturally stealthy. I sneak up on people by accident all the time." Avery walked over and peeked around Quinn to the nightstand. "Your phone isn't on. Were you talking to yourself?"

"No, I'm not weird or anything." Quinn glanced down at the egg and back up at Avery.

Avery's gaze followed Quinn's eyes. "Is that what I think it is?"

"That depends. What do you think it is?" Quinn asked.

"It looks like a dragon egg," Avery replied. "A variety of chromatic green from the look of it."

"How do you know all this stuff, but you can't pick up on all the clues I've been dropping about you being here?"

Avery shrugged. "I had to study a lot about supernatural creatures growing up. It was required reading, and Gemma would test me on it all the time. As to the other, I guess I'm not that good at reading people. I've never hung around other girls my own age before."

"Well, obviously," Quinn said, rolling her eyes. She realized her tone was harsh and regretted it. "Look, I'm sorry. I'm sore and tired."

Avery smiled and sat down with the dragon egg between them. Quinn's floral shampoo smelled nice in the other girl's hair.

"It's okay if you were talking to the egg. I have an old steel helmet in my room at the castle. It's been sitting in the windowsill since I was little, maybe for hundreds of years. I drew eyes on it once with charcoal from the fireplace, so it didn't feel so weird when I talked to it. Sometimes I feel like it's my only friend in the world."

Quinn smiled, trying to picture Avery chatting with a rusty old helmet.

Avery returned the smile and said, "Great, now you think *I'm* the crazy one."

"No, I was just thinking about how much you and I are suddenly alike when I didn't think there was any way we could be."

"At least you're talking to something that could be alive, potentially. Mine is somebody's medieval trash left behind in the room I call home."

"You said you lived in a castle?" Quinn asked. "That must be pretty cool."

"If by cool you mean damp and chilly, then yes, it's cool. Gemma found a warded fortress in the Pyrenees mountains between France and Spain. She took me there to be safe during the purges. I never knew my parents. I was too young."

Quinn shrugged. "Me either, at least not until recently. I never knew my dad. They put me up for adoption when I was a baby."

"But isn't Naomi your mother? Having a vampire for a mother must be—"

"Fun?" Quinn replied. "Not really. We've only just reconnected. I'm still trying to figure out what we are to each other. Mostly she just finds ways to make my life miserable, usually with new training challenges."

"You mean like Gemma does?"

Their eyes met, and they burst out laughing.

After a minute, Quinn wiped her eyes. "I guess mothers come in all types and sizes."

"Agreed. But she's more than just my mother; she's my

guide in this quest for the prophecy, too. Sometimes I wish I had a friend like Taylor. I've seen the two of you talking. You seem very close."

Quinn nodded. "Taylor was there for me when I really needed someone. She sort of rescued me from what I might have become while I was living on the street."

"What was that?"

"A punk petty criminal, or maybe a member of one of the gangs that plague the city. I could see either or maybe both happening if it hadn't been for her."

Avery shuddered. "Even though I know how to defend myself, I can't imagine what it must've been like, living out there all alone."

Quinn's hand drifted up to her amulet, stroking the engraved wolf's head on the silver oval. "I wasn't really alone, although I didn't know it at the time. Between the protective magic of the Hunter amulet they left with me and a secret motherly vampire watching over me, I was probably safer than anyone else out there."

"But you didn't know it at the time. I imagine it was scary."

"Yeah, a little."

"I wish I had an amulet like yours, but Gemma didn't have the necessary magic to create one for me. Where'd you get that one?"

"It was originally my mother's. She gave it to me when she left me on the steps of a firehouse during the purges." Quinn shrugged. "I guess giving up some of her magical protection to me was a way of taking care of me when she couldn't be there."

"I don't know who my parents are," Avery said. She

stared to the side, looking out the window at the night sky. "I would love to find out one or both of them were still alive out there, somewhere. You're lucky."

Quinn started to make a comment around being careful what you wish for, but she stopped. Naomi wasn't all that bad, despite the way she treated the woman sometimes. She still didn't think of her as her mother, but there were moments now when she felt closer to the vampire than she had at first.

Quinn smiled, "At least your mother isn't nearly the same age as you like mine is. Since Naomi stopped aging when they turned her, she only looks a few years older than I am. That causes all sorts of problems out in public and kind of messes with my head."

"How did you find out she was alive?" Avery asked. "It must've been a shock."

"We almost fought the first few times we met," Quinn said with a grin. "At least, I almost fought her. I didn't realize it at first, but she always avoided fighting me in those first few encounters."

Quinn shared how she and her mother first met while she was in the employ of the vampire John Handon.

Avery listened, leaning forward and hanging on every word. The way she became so engaged in the story seemed strange to Quinn, and more than a little annoying.

When Quinn finished telling her about the final battle to free her mother and the others, Avery shook her head and said, "Wow, that is incredible. I would love to know what it's like to fight real vampires or werewolves. You're so lucky."

"Wait, you've never faced any?"

Avery shook her head. "No, Gemma only recently took me out of the castle to come here. Before that, it was all training and study."

"Who else was in the castle? It wasn't just the two of you, was it?"

"Oh, no, Gemma had visitors frequently, though I only saw a few of them. Those were the ones who came to train me in combat or magic use. Most of the others were members of the Fae court, I think. I caught glimpses of some of them when I got bored and practiced my spying and hiding skills around the castle."

"Fae?" Quinn asked. For some reason, the revelation raised alarm bells in her mind. "What kind of Fae?"

"I gathered they were nobility of some sort. I only figured it out because of the way Gemma would address them when she greeted them. Most often, it was a princess or duke, folks like that."

"And you never met them?" Quinn asked. "These Fae princesses and dukes?"

"No," Avery said. "None of them except for Princess Filippa. But she was one of the people who trained me, so I never considered her that way. I didn't know she was a princess until I overheard one of the others address her as such."

Now the alarms in Quinn's head made sense. She got up and walked over to stare out the window while she tried to make sense of this. If Filippa was involved, that made Avery and Gemma trouble for Quinn and the others in the clan.

Quinn turned back to Avery and faked a yawn. "I think

I'm going to hit the sack. You're all right out there, aren't you?"

Avery nodded. "Sure. Is everything good with you? I feel like I said something to upset you."

"No," Quinn lied. "Everything's fine. Just a little tired, that's all."

Avery went to the living room. It all made sense now. Filippa had to be behind all this; she only had to figure out how. She picked up her phone and started to tap a message to Clark and the others, but stopped and put it down. Taylor might believe her, but Clark, Naomi, and Miranda wouldn't. They didn't see the Fae, or at least some of them, as a threat.

Leaning back in bed against her pillows, Quinn stared up at the water-stained plaster on the ceiling and tried to come up with some way to find out what was really going on. Only then could she expose Avery and Gemma as the frauds they were.

CHAPTER TEN

Since Clark and Naomi wouldn't take her suspicions about the Fae seriously, Quinn decided she had to rely on other resources. The next day was scheduled for rest to give the girls a chance to heal from their non-stop bouts. It was the perfect opportunity for Quinn to slip away and get some of her questions answered.

Right after breakfast, Quinn followed Taylor back into her office area by the storerooms, avoiding the others.

Taylor smiled as Quinn came into the room with her. "You gonna hang with me today? I have a lot to work on with upgrades to the system and Miranda's magic training, but you're welcome to watch."

"I can for a little bit, but I was hoping you'd cover for me if anyone comes around asking where I am."

Taylor cocked her head to the side. "What's up? You have that sneaky look on your face."

"I need to investigate some stuff Avery had been telling me about how she grew up." Quinn paused, then decided to bring Taylor in on her suspicions. "She mentioned Filippa,

T. I think that Fae woman is trying to cause trouble to get back at me for imprinting the dragon egg."

"You sure, Quinn? You know Clark and Naomi think she's just a typical self-absorbed Fae who doesn't care about any of us humans. She's not really out to get you. She doesn't give a damn about any of us."

"You don't have to believe me. Just tell the others I went downtown to go shopping or something."

Taylor shrugged. "I can do that, I guess. Where will you really be?"

"I'm going to talk to Aurora. She's staying somewhere in the city. She doesn't like Filippa, so maybe I can find out if she knows anything about Gemma or Avery, or what Filippa has planned for them."

"If you want, I can do some digging on my end, too. There has to be a record of what Gemma was up to with Avery in Europe. I'll see what I can find while you're out."

"Thanks, T. I knew I could count on you."

"Always," Taylor said. "Don't be too late getting back, though. Clark will get bent out of shape if he thinks you're out partying or something."

"It shouldn't take too long. I'll keep you in the loop and check in when I can."

Quinn left Taylor's office and turned left down the long underground hallway, heading away from O'Malley's instead of to the bar. She'd use one of the other exits from the tunnel system instead of taking the chance Clark or Naomi would catch her leaving.

Once she reached the street, she caught a bus downtown, then pulled out her phone and sent a message to Princess Aurora. She was one of the only Fae who paid any attention to human technology. The princess had been mostly friendly to Quinn and the others. She might be willing to part with information about Filippa.

Quinn didn't have to wait long. A message pinged back with an address off Charles Street in the Mount Vernon area of the city. Quinn figured she was about a half-hour away, depending on the bus schedule. For a moment she thought about catching a cab, but she didn't have a lot of money. She hadn't asked Clark for anything additional recently, even though he'd offered to supplement what he gave her from the Hunter resources they still had.

She replied, sending a message that she'd be there soon. Quinn slipped the phone into her pocket and headed over a few blocks to catch one of the uptown buses heading toward the Mt. Vernon district.

Thirty minutes later, Quinn stood on the street and double-checked the location on her phone. The three-story stone and brick house seemed much like all the others in the neighborhood. There was nothing that designated it as the city home of Fae royalty.

She laughed to herself. What did she expect, some sort of magical flag or glowing emblem on the door? On a whim, Quinn pulled up her HUD. There was the pentagram icon of her new Arcane Sight ability. Activating it, Quinn stared at the building.

Some areas glowed with magical energy. They weren't loose fragments of natural magic that floated by her as she stood there. That indicated they were completed spells, or maybe wards of some sort.

Letting the magical spectrum slip away, she headed up the steps. Quinn reached for the brass knocker but didn't quite get there. The door opened inward on its own, revealing a tall Fae male with light-brown hair and just the hint of his pointed ears peeking out from the curled locks on either side of his head.

"Hello, Zephyr," Quinn said with a nod to the princess's head of security. "I believe her Highness is expecting me?"

"She is. You're running a little late, though."

"Hey, blame the MTA. I don't control the buses around here."

"Indeed," Zephyr said as if not accepting her excuse entirely. "If you'll come this way." The guard gestured inside and closed the door behind her before taking the lead, with Quinn close behind him.

He walked to an atrium at the rear of the building. Potted plants covered most of the floor, and more hung from overhead hooks. It all made Quinn feel like she was in some sort of rainforest exhibit at the zoo. She even spotted small songbirds flitting amidst the greenery.

Princess Aurora sat in a white wicker chair with a high back. There was an identical chair beside her, with a small matching table in between. A silver tray with a tall glass pitcher of what looked like pale white wine sat atop the table.

As Quinn approached, following Zephyr, Aurora looked up and smiled. She picked up an empty crystal wine glass and filled it from the pitcher, placing it on the table beside the empty chair.

"Quinn, my dear, please do come and sit down. It's always a pleasure to see you. How's my egg doing?"

"Um, fine, I guess," Quinn said. She didn't say anything

about how it seemed to respond to her talks with it. "How are you?"

"I'm very well, of course. Everything in the city is so much better without all that nonsense from John Handon and his coven getting in the way. It was nice of you to take care of that for us."

"Just another service from your friendly neighborhood Huntress clan, I guess." Quinn sat down but didn't pick up the wine glass. Instead, she folded her hands in her lap and glanced at the nearby plants. She couldn't shake the feeling that someone or something watched her from behind all that greenery.

Aurora turned to her head of security after a moment of awkward silence. "Zephyr, be a darling and give us some time. I think we can trust our Huntress friend to behave without you around."

"As you wish, Your Highness." The tall bodyguard nodded and pivoted in place one hundred eighty degrees before exiting the room. As he left, he pulled the French doors closed behind him.

Quinn could still see him through the glass in the doors. He walked over and took up a position in the hallway against the far wall where he could keep an eye on Quinn and the princess.

"We are alone now, Quinn. Why don't you tell me what brought you over here? I assume it wasn't to chat about the weather. Is it something to do with my dragon egg?"

"Oh, no, the egg is fine. I mean, nothing weird has happened if that's what you're asking." Quinn shut her mouth, feeling like she'd said enough. She worried that the

Fae would see through her deception and want to know more about the egg.

"Then what is it, my dear? I certainly don't mind receiving visitors from time to time, but I have other things to do with my time."

"Of course you do," Quinn said. She stood up and crossed to a cluster of low shrubs and ferns in large terra-cotta planters. She stared into the leaves for a few seconds, distracted because she'd just seen a flicker of movement.

"Quinn, if you don't tell me what is bothering you, I cannot help you."

Pulling her attention back to the matter at hand, the Huntress decided a direct approach was best. Screwing up her courage, she said, "It's about Filippa. You heard about her involvement during my final confrontation with Handon?"

"I did hear a few things. My understanding was she was observing some rather distasteful ceremonies. Honestly, she always did have a thing for the macabre."

"She stood by while that monster tried to kill my friend and me. She should have—"

"Should have what? Intervened? It's my understanding she was alone, without her attendants or guards. What would you have had her do?"

Quinn started to answer and stopped, shutting her mouth and biting her lip as she tried to come up with an answer. She knew Filippa was working against her. The evidence was all circumstantial, but there was a lot of it.

Finally, she broke the silence. "I don't know, but that's not the only time she's worked on things that undermined what my friends and I are doing. You know that all too well. That was how we met."

Aurora smiled. "You merely got caught up in a little tug-of-war between factions in the Fae hierarchy, Quinn. That's all. The rest is coincidence, I'm sure. Has she done something else since the Handon incident?"

"Yes, as a matter of fact, she has. She has apparently been grooming her own Huntress this whole time in Europe somewhere. Now that girl is here with her handler and wants to take everything over."

"So, my cousin kept that little project going after all. I thought she'd lost interest in that alternate version of the prophecy. It's just the one who showed up, or were there more?"

"Filippa has more than one Huntress in training?" Quinn asked, alarmed at the prospect.

"I honestly don't know. I thought she'd lost interest in that particular set of endeavors years ago."

"So, you know about Avery and Gemma?"

"Gemma Beckinglsy? That's who Filippa got to head up her little project?" Aurora chuckled and nodded. "It makes sense. She was an accomplished Hunter clan mage before the purges, despite her youth. Since she survived them, she must be even more powerful now. And this Avery? Is she your counterpart?"

Quinn nodded, saying, "She is, and she is just so…"

When Quinn's voice trailed off before finishing her description, a hint of a grin played across Aurora's lips. "I see."

"You see what?"

"It's not easy to find yourself respecting someone who is your rival. Believe me, I know."

"I don't respect her," Quinn snapped.

Aurora studied her face for a few seconds, and her smile broadened. "You don't just respect her. You're attracted to her, aren't you? My, my, that lends a wrinkle to things, doesn't it?"

Quinn started to deny it, but the twinkle in the Fae princess's eyes stopped her. There was no hiding it. The woman had seen straight through her. Did that mean everyone knew, even Avery?

As if reading her mind, Aurora said, "Oh, don't worry. I have a way of getting that sort of information out of people. I'm a distant relative of Cupid, you know."

Trying to decide if she was kidding or not, Quinn remembered something else the woman had said. "What was that you said about an alternate prophecy? You said Filippa was using a different prediction, one of her own?"

"It's not a different prophecy, darling. It's more or less a different translation of the same prophecy."

"That doesn't make any sense," Quinn replied. "I heard the words from the clan leaders themselves. Wouldn't they know the correct translation? It *is* a Hunter prophecy, after all."

Quinn cleared her throat and recited the words spoken to her during her confrontation with Handon in the ceremonial chamber.

"For in time will come one who was lost.
They will restore that which was taken.
They will rebuild the clans.
Forging them into the final weapon."

"Interesting," Aurora said. "I knew the Hunters had a different version, but I had never heard it."

"What's in the other version that makes it so different? This one seems pretty clear to me."

"Come back and sit down. Have a drink. I have to go and find a certain book in my library. I want to be sure to get it right."

Quinn returned to her seat, but when the princess gestured to the wine glass, she shook her head. "I don't really care for wine."

"Oh, don't worry about that. It's ambrosia, a mixture of rare fruit juices and honey. Try it. It's my personal family recipe."

The woman left Quinn alone, pulling open the French doors and disappearing down a side hallway. Zephyr still stood at his post against the opposite wall outside. His eyes never left Quinn.

She offered the guard a brief smile, then lifted the wineglass and sniffed the pale liquid inside. It smelled delicious—fruity, but with alien floral scents as well. Quinn took a cautious sip and then stared down at the glass with a huge smile on her face. It wasn't just good, it was wonderful and delicious, possibly the best drink she'd ever had.

Quinn finished her glass and was in the process of pouring herself another from the decanter when Aurora returned.

"It's very good, isn't it? I'm sorry I didn't tell you what it was when you first arrived. It was foolish of me to not realize you didn't know the custom for a meeting like this one. It would never do to serve spirits or anything that could cloud the mind when meeting with a person of equal rank like this."

Quinn started to say thank you and stopped. "Wait, you think of me as equal in rank? I'm not a princess or anything like that."

"You're a clan leader, a proven warrior, deemed worthy by a dragon egg, and the potential embodiment of an ancient prophecy. I think that qualifies, don't you?" Aurora's eyes glinted with amusement.

Quinn wasn't sure if the Fae was teasing her. After a few seconds, she decided the princess was being sincere. She nodded. "Thank you then. Is that the book?"

Aurora held up a small leather-bound book about an inch thick. Its size surprised Quinn. For something like this, she had expected a magnificent volume full of prophecies.

The princess flipped open the book, revealing pages of handwritten lines in a language she didn't recognize. Even some of the alphabet looked alien. From the way the other woman traced her hands down the pages, the text moved from right to left instead of the opposite way, as in English books.

After flipping through a few more pages, she stopped. "Ah, here it is. I knew I'd written it down."

Aurora leaned forward, holding the book so Quinn could see, even though she couldn't read it. The lines of script had doodles of flowers and what looked like hats and dresses in the margins.

"This is my journal from when I was younger. One of my instructors was always going on about this prophecy and the arguments about what it meant."

"Why is there a disagreement? A translation should be straightforward, right?"

"The two are translations of a translation, a copy of a copy if you will. The final copy will not be as true to the original as the first copy was. Each additional copy down the line will be slightly different, no matter how careful you are."

"Well, let's go back to the original, then," Quinn said.

Aurora shook her head. "The original is not of this world. It came from a single page of a book in the demon realm. Long ago, a rebel escaped with a copy of it and brought it to the Fae on this world, claiming it was the secret to foiling plans to take over the Earthly plane."

"You said, 'long ago.' When was this?"

"Sometime around 1300 BC if I remember my instructor's ramblings about it." She glanced at the text on the page and continued, "Here it is. He was the court mage to Queen Nefertiti when a nearly-dead demon spawn, the half-human child of a man and a female demon, stumbled from the central passage of one of the great pyramids near Giza."

Aurora read on, flipping the page. "Guards brought him to the court of Nefertiti, and he was interviewed by the queen's advisors, who tried to understand his fevered ramblings. He died soon after he was discovered, but they managed to recover the scrap of parchment he clutched and decipher the text written there."

"Why the two versions if they had the original parchment?" Quinn asked.

"The queen's advisors had two differing interpretations. One ascribed the prophecy to champions to come sometime in the future who would help gather the Fae under a single ruler once and for all. The other, tendered by a few of the human scholars in the council, said it referred to mankind, not the Fae. They thought it meant it would be the leader of a select group or clan of humans who would ultimately defeat the final incursion of demonkind."

Quinn asked, "I know what my version said. What was the version the Fae mage came up with?"

Aurora glanced down at her notes and frowned. "Since you don't speak Fae, I'll have to translate the archaic tongue to English for you."

She considered the page for a few seconds, then said,

"At the end will come the ones who were lost.

They will restore that which was broken.

Rebuilding the brotherhood.

Melding them under the last conqueror."

Quinn shook her head. "The two don't sound like the same thing at all. Your version doesn't even talk about defeating the demons."

"Of course not," Aurora said, eyebrows raised in shock. "We couldn't reunite under a single ruler if we destroyed our cousins from the netherworld."

Quinn nearly spluttered ambrosia through her nose. "'Cousins?' What does that mean?"

"Oh, dear, you don't know, do you." The princess sighed and closed the book in her lap. "The Fae and demonkind were one race before a war split the two factions and banished the losers to the lower planes. Ever since, they've tried to find a way to return and cast out their oppressors. The prophecy speaks of that return and of the possibility that our two factions might someday reunite."

"What about that conqueror part? That sounds ominous."

"There are those among the Fae who assume we will ascend to control this plane someday."

Quinn didn't like the sound of that. She didn't press the issue with the princess, though. What would be the point? She'd come to find out what Filippa was up to with Avery and Gemma. At least, she now knew a little about what was driving her to interfere with Quinn and her friends.

Standing, Quinn smiled at Aurora. "Thank you for taking the time to explain all this to me. It's given me a lot to think about."

"I'm always happy to make time to assist you, Quinn. I think there are many important matters hinging on your decisions right now."

Aurora rose and walked Quinn to the front door. Zephyr, who had followed them, pulled it open and held it as Quinn stepped through to stand on the stoop.

"Take care of my dragon egg, dear. I have my calendar marked for when you can bring it back to me."

"I'll make sure it is safe and sound. Don't worry," the Huntress said.

Quinn headed down the steps and back toward the bus stop. She had a lot on her mind and more questions now than when she left. It was time to make a plan for what to do next.

CHAPTER ELEVEN

I t was lunchtime when Quinn arrived back at O'Malley's. She'd hoped to slide through the busy lunch crowd without being seen and go find Taylor in the back rooms.

No such luck.

"Quinn," Avery called. "Over here."

Forcing herself to smile and hide the anger she held inside at the information she'd found about Filippa, Quinn walked over to the bar. Avery sat on the stool in front of a pub burger that set Quinn's mouth to watering.

"Taylor said you went shopping." Avery glanced down at Quinn's empty hands. "Didn't you find anything? Maybe I can come with you if you go back out this afternoon. Shopping sounds fun, and I'd love to help you find whatever you were looking for."

"I'm not sure I'm going back out. It wasn't all that urgent." Quinn scanned the crowded club. "Have you seen Taylor, or maybe Clark and Naomi?"

"Your friend is back in her computer lab. I just found

out you call her the tech witch. That's spectacular. It defines her from top to bottom."

"That's sort of the point," Quinn said. She couldn't resist a snarky addition. "It's what a nickname does, after all."

"I know that, but it's not something Gemma does. Giving a colleague a nickname is something that seems so friendly, personal. Gemma never does anything without a purpose. There's no room in her plans for that sort of frivolity."

"That's a shame." Quinn tried to keep her answer short and looked around, avoiding making eye contact. She figured if she didn't engage with the other girl, she'd lose interest and let Quinn go find Taylor and the others.

"I know!" Avery exclaimed, her eyes bright with excitement. "You can give me a nickname. It would be perfect coming from you."

How about two-faced? Quinn thought. She held the forced smile on her face and said, "That's not the way it works, Avery. A nickname comes from something specific, from a particular thing you do at a certain time that stands out."

"Of course. I only thought you might... Well, never mind. I suppose it will come in its own time."

"That's the spirit," Quinn replied, happy Avery was letting that particular thought go. She was so strange. As a warrior, she was incredible, something Quinn hated to admit. But in social situations and in one-on-one conversations like this, she was like a little kid. She remembered what the girl told her about how Gemma had trained her in isolation growing up. Quinn almost felt sorry for her. Almost.

"Hey, look, I've gotta go find Taylor. You should finish that burger before it gets cold. We'll be back at the training tomorrow, don't forget."

"I don't think so. Gemma has something she and I need to do."

"Oh?" Quinn asked. Avery had mentioned something earlier about Gemma's plans. "What's that?"

"Ummm, I'm not sure." Avery looked away. "Just something Gemma has to do while we're in town. That's all."

Quinn knew the other girl was hiding something. It increased her suspicions about their involvement with the missing werebadgers. She had to get to Taylor.

"Ummm, yeah, that's good," Quinn said. "We'll have another day off. Enjoy your lunch."

Quinn left Avery sitting at the bar and wove through the tables to the door to the storerooms. A quick jaunt down the long hallway took her to Taylor's workroom. She poked her head inside to see if her friend was there.

Taylor was hunched over the table they had set up for the VR system, working on something. Miranda's ghostly form hovered beside her, intent on what the tech witch was doing. They both looked up when Quinn peeked in.

"Hey, how'd your 'shopping trip' go?" Taylor asked.

Quinn glanced at Miranda and said, "I found part of what I was looking for, but now I need your help with, uh, some online shopping."

Miranda smiled. "Goodness, you two are the worst at keeping secrets. I can tell you're up to something. First of all, you hate shopping, Quinn. You talk about it all the time. What were you really doing all morning?"

Taylor tried to cover. "No, she really had to get some stuff. I told you."

"Taylor," Miranda said. "One of the things I most adore about you is how painfully honest you are. You're the worst liar I've ever seen." Miranda turned back to Quinn. "Come in and close the door, then tell me what you've really been up to."

Quinn came in and pushed the door shut, deciding she had nothing to lose. "I went to visit Princess Aurora downtown. I had questions for her after I learned there might be a connection between Avery's sudden arrival here and Filippa."

Miranda's eyebrows shot up. "Really? That can't be good."

Taylor nodded. "Exactly. That's why Quinn had to go and find out what she might be up to."

"Have you told your mother or Clark?" Miranda asked. "They'll want to know if something is up."

Quinn shook her head. "They only want to prove I have the training to be a better Huntress than the new girl in town. If I'm going to bring this to them, I need more than a casual mention of that Fae backstabber in a single conversation. That's why I went to Aurora. I'm glad I did because I ended up uncovering a whole other thing we have to worry about."

"What's that?" Taylor asked.

"There's another version of the Huntress prophecy, one that has important implications for the Fae." Quinn went on to explain what she'd learned from Aurora.

When she finished, she shrugged and said, "That's why I need to figure out what Gemma's here to do with Avery. It's not whatever she's telling Clark and Naomi. It has nothing to do with challenging me. I need to know the real reason before I can go to them."

"You should give them more credit," Miranda said. "They've been around a lot longer than you have, and I'm sure they know all about Fae trickery and what Filippa's capable of."

"I don't think so," Quinn shot back. "Clark's got a blind spot where Filippa's concerned, given his history with her, and I still don't trust Naomi. That's why I'm hoping Taylor can help me investigate my suspicions and get more evidence about what Gemma and Filippa are up to."

"What about Avery?" Taylor asked. "She's got to be involved, too."

"Maybe," Quinn replied. "But I don't think she's in on the whole plot. She's a worse liar than you are, and I don't think she's aware of how treacherous Gemma and Filippa are."

"You flipped your opinion of Avery pretty fast since the last time you talked to me about her."

"I don't know, T," Quinn said. "There's a lot about her that's so sheltered. She just does whatever Gemma tells her to without question. That's a problem, but I don't think she's as guilty as the other two. I need to find out for sure, though, so what do you think?"

"I do like to unravel a mystery. Miranda? We could use your knowledge of magic and Fae influence."

Miranda thought about it for a few seconds and

nodded. "I will help, but only if you promise to take whatever we find out to Clark and Naomi. Deal?"

Quinn and Taylor replied in unison, "Deal."

"Well, then," Miranda said. "Where do we start? You must have some thoughts, Quinn."

"I do. First, we need to search for anything about the Fae version of the prophecy. There must be a Baltimore connection somehow, or they wouldn't have come here."

"That's a bit of a stretch," Taylor said. "Didn't you say this happened like three thousand years ago?"

"Yes, but the Fae might have been on this continent back then and left something behind, or maybe they brought something with them when they arrived with the rest of the settlers who built the city."

Taylor sat down in the chair behind her triple monitors, pulled the wireless keyboard into her lap, and started typing. "Let's see what we can find out. Tell me the Fae version of the prophecy again so I can enter it, then we'll see if we can backtrack it to Fae language keywords to search."

"When did you learn to speak Fae, T?" Quinn asked.

"I didn't, but I was able to load a translator program and, with Miranda's help, used a spell to add magical and mystic languages to the database. We should be able to do a search using that."

"What? There's a Fae version of the internet?" Quinn queried.

"There is. It's located on the dark web, of course, but that won't stop me." Taylor grinned. "What's the version of the prophecy you got from Aurora? Try to be exact. It could make a difference."

Quinn recited Aurora's version to Taylor while her friend entered it. As soon as she finished speaking, Taylor went to work. At one point, she stopped tapping and started chanting rhythmically while she wriggled her fingers over the keyboard.

When the tech witch finished chanting and started typing again, Quinn asked, "Was that a spell?"

"Yeah, there's a whole part of the web hidden from even the best human hackers. Miranda and I found it by accident when we were doing some of the work to get the new VirSync gear integrated into our homemade system. I used a magical password spell to get me in. Now we can start searching for Fae keywords. First, though, I need to reverse-translate what you told me in English."

Quinn watched as the tech witch did her thing. The three screens now had a blue-green glow emanating from them as lines of code, images, and text flashed by. Some of the graphics depicted various creatures from the supernatural realm. A few she recognized, but many she didn't, highlighting how much she still had to learn about this world full of mythical creatures.

It took Taylor about twenty minutes to get the translation to the Fae language completed. The runic alphabet on the screen was illegible as far as Quinn was concerned.

"Don't worry," Taylor assured her. "I did the reverse-translation a second time using a different translator. It came out very close to what you told me to begin with. I think it's as close as we're going to get."

"So, now what? You start searching using those weird letters and words?"

Miranda nodded. "Taylor should be able to use the

magical interface to comb through the Fae records we've found so far, as well as potentially uncover others. There's a lot we don't know about yet, I'm sure."

Quinn sat down in a nearby chair where she could see the monitors. "I guess I wait, then. I don't want to wander around out there. I might run into Clark or Naomi. With my luck, they'd decide to run me through some training bouts to give me extra incentive to beat Avery the next time we meet."

Taylor laughed. "Like you need anyone to make you more competitive than you already are."

Quinn smiled. Taylor knew her better than anyone else. "Keep your eyes on the prize, please. I want to find out what Filippa's up to."

"Yes, Mistress Huntress, ma'am." Taylor turned back to her work, chuckling.

Quinn settled back and let Taylor and Miranda work. The amount of help Miranda offered as Taylor ran her search surprised Quinn. Although she thought this would be more tech than magic, and outside of the ghost's expertise, Miranda offered Taylor a lot of little tweaks and insights as she worked through the process.

It took Taylor and Miranda the afternoon and well into the evening to finally start yielding answers to what Quinn hoped to find. While they were working, she took a chance and snuck out to find Juni, who was in the kitchen. She arranged to have snacks and drinks brought in every few hours while the tech witch worked.

Taylor got distracted when she dug into a project like this. She often forgot to eat or drink anything except for the occasional energy drink. With the leprechaun's help,

Quinn managed to get her friend to eat a patty melt and some fries. Later, they brought her some hot wings, and she nibbled on those as she continued her deep dive into the Fae web.

Around nine, Taylor leaned back in her seat, stretched her arms out to the sides and smiled at Quinn.

"Who's the best Fae web hacker around?" Taylor brought her hands back in with her thumbs pointed at her chest. "That's right. It's this gal."

"Did you find anything?" Quinn asked, getting up and moving over to stand behind Taylor. She stared at the monitors, but there was nothing on the screen except runes and ancient things that sort of looked like hieroglyphics.

Quinn pointed at the things that looked like Egyptian drawings. "Those look like they're from a mummy movie."

"You're not far off," Taylor said. "I tracked this back to references that are very old. Those are scans of Egyptian accounts dating back to about the time to which Aurora referred. From what I can discern from them and the Fae historian's commentary about what was written, something else was brought to this world by the hybrid demon. It was used to create a magical artifact of power."

"That's what Filippa is looking for?" Quinn asked.

"Maybe," Miranda said. The ghost pointed to the middle screen, which was filled with runes arraigned in paragraphs. "That's why this part is important, too. They are several references to a powerful tool used to create a well in the New World."

"A well? Like, a hole in the ground?"

"Maybe," Taylor said. "The translation might not have it

correct. I'm not sure it makes sense in English, but it's the best I could come up with. Either way, this well exists." She pointed to an old, yellow map of the North American coastline from Greenland down to the Caribbean. "This map was included with one of the references. It shows the locations of several magical terminals or loci here along the coast. Each of them is a major focal point of power, either a ley line or another source."

Taylor moved her fingers across her touchpad, and the map zoomed in. Quinn saw pentagram stars inside circles marked up and down the coastline. Taylor stopped so the map centered on the mid-Atlantic area. She tapped the monitor over one of the stars and smiled at Quinn.

"Is that nearby?" the Huntress asked.

"From this map, which dates back to the late 1600s, it is somewhere beneath the original city. I can't tell exactly where, but it must be near the water since there hadn't been too much exploration inland at that point."

Quinn nodded. Things were starting to click into place. "That's why Avery was there intimidating Inez, the were-badger leader."

Taylor cocked her head to the side in an unspoken question.

"You said it yourself. The power center or well or whatever it is lies *beneath* the city. It's underground. That's why they need the badger shifters. They're natural miners, and they're not very social. No one would necessarily notice when some of them went missing."

"If that's true, then you and Clark were onto something when you decided to go over there and talk to Inez. Then Avery showed up and got her to clam up."

Quinn nodded. "I'd be willing to bet Gemma and Avery have been in the city for a while, maybe weeks longer than we've been aware of their presence. I'm sure they are tied to the werebadger disappearances. If we track them down, I think we'll find this well or whatever it is."

Quinn pointed to the table with the VR rig. "Send me back to the restaurant so I can talk to the matriarch again. She needs to tell me what's going on. Maybe I can convince her."

"What if she won't?" Miranda asked.

Quinn answered with a grim smile. "Failure isn't an option at this point. If Filippa's looking for something, that makes it vitally important to us, too."

She climbed onto the table and laid down, then settled the headset and goggles in place. "Do it."

Taylor hesitated, then nodded and ran through a quick-start process. The VR system and gear started humming. Quinn closed her eyes as she fell backward into blackness once again.

CHAPTER TWELVE

Quinn came out of the darkness in a crouch on one knee, shaking off the intense sensation of the VR transition. She was glad they had finally gotten their hands on the most up-to-date VirSync gear. The nausea and headaches were almost completely absent with the new rig.

Tapping her ear, Quinn said, "I'm here. The parking lot is mostly empty."

"I'm not surprised," Taylor said over the comm. "It's almost 10. The restaurant is probably closing soon if it hasn't already."

"I'd better get over there and see what I can find out then. I'll touch base when I'm ready to return."

"Good luck," Taylor said.

Quinn disconnected and stood up, scanning the area for any sign of trouble. Starting toward the restaurant, Quinn muttered "mist" and disappeared into the shadows. The hazy, slightly-out-of-focus ring around her visual field told her the Huntress skill was engaged.

She reached the rear entrance to the kitchen, where a screen door allowed the banging of pots and pans inside to drift outside. The noise told her people were in there, but she couldn't see how many from this angle.

Quinn pulled the door open just enough to let her slip inside and let it close behind her. She winced at the slight squeak of the hinges as it slowly shut. Quinn moved to the side and stood against the wall beside a tall shelf of canned goods. She got out of the way just in time.

A small man with the hairiest arms she'd ever seen came around the corner and stared at the screen door. "Hey, did you hear the door open, Charlie?"

A voice from the end of the kitchen responded, "I can't hear a damned thing over this dishwasher. Who is it?"

"That's just it. There's no one there." The man walked over to the door and looked out at the parking lot. He stood there, sniffing and watching. Quinn caught a hint of moist earth and damp fur. He was one of the werebadgers. He kept sniffing the air coming in from the parking lot. After a minute or so, he hmphed and headed back around the corner.

Quinn realized she'd been holding her breath the whole time he'd been standing there. She let it out in a long, slow sigh.

"Did you find anything, Chet?" Charlie asked.

"No, but I smelled something. I couldn't nail down what or who it was, but I swear someone was there."

"You've been up too long. Didn't you work the breakfast rush, too?"

"Yeah, somebody has to. I don't see you getting up at four-thirty to come in and open the kitchen."

"That's because I have a life."

"Wait and see what happens when you get old like me. You can't sleep right, can't pee right, can't do anything right anymore. All you have to look forward to is work, work, work."

"God help me when I get old enough to have all that happen to me. I'd be better off working in the tunnels like the others. At least then, I'd end up making some money while I'm wasting away."

"Don't say that, Charlie. I know a lot of you youngsters got caught up working for that crazy lady, but working in a hole like that is hard, dangerous work. A lot of our kin never came home from their jobs. This one is worse than most, from what I hear. That witch is trying to hide it from everyone in the city while pushing everyone to dig faster. That means she is cutting corners on safety, too, most likely."

"At least it's better than coming here to wash dishes every night. She did promise she'd pay those of us she took for the work."

"Dishwashing gets you home safe and sound. Don't you have a cute little girlfriend now?"

Quinn slid from behind the shelf of canned goods and peeked around the corner. The kitchen ran down a long ten-foot-wide rectangle for about twenty feet. The grill and oven ran along the wall nearest to the parking lot. Behind that in the middle was a long steel table with shelves to hold the dishes ready for the servers to pick up.

Against the wall farthest from Quinn and the entrance was a triple sink next to a commercial dishwasher station. A man stood with his back to her, spraying plates and stacking them in a plastic rack to slide into the washers when it was ready. That must be Charlie.

Chet stood at the stovetop, stacking saucepans and other cooking utensils and carrying them over to Charlie. Once that was finished, he started wiping down the long steel table and all the shelves.

A woman's voice came from the restaurant proper and in through a swinging door walked Inez. "Charlie, Chet, you two almost finished back here? I wanna get home."

Charlie looked over his shoulder, "We're almost finished. Chet heard a ghost and had to go check to make sure they stayed out in the parking lot."

Inez shot a glance in Quinn's direction, staring past her at the door before looking back at the two kitchen workers. "What exactly did you hear?"

"I thought the door opened, but there was no one there when I went to check. I thought I smelled something—lavender, of all things. But it was faint and I couldn't see anyone, so I figured it was nothing."

Quinn raised her hand to her hair, twisting a stray lock at her temple around her index finger. Her shampoo was lavender-scented. Her shadow-hiding ability made her nearly invisible but didn't cover her smell from anyone sensitive enough to detect it.

The old woman sniffed the air twice, wrinkling her nose. She stared past Quinn at the screen door one more time for a few seconds, then shook her head. "Hurry up and finish up in here. I'll be down in my office, finishing the register count. Let me know when you're done."

The two men nodded and went back to work cleaning up the kitchen. Inez went through another open door nearby and down a flight of stairs into the basement. Quinn waited ten seconds and checked the two men to make sure they didn't see her. Once it was clear, she darted to the basement steps and headed down.

The bottom of the stairs opened up into more storage, with metal shelves in rows with various canned goods, boxes, and restaurant pans and utensils. A doorway opened to the left of the stairs.

The door was ajar, and Inez's voice filtered out as Quinn reached the bottom step. "If you're dumb enough to come down here, girl, after you knew I could smell ya upstairs, it must be important."

Quinn peeked around the doorframe to find Inez seated in an old metal desk chair. She leaned back and stared at the doorway.

"I know you're there. Show yourself."

Sighing, Quinn ticked the icon in the HUD that cleared her hiding ability. The hazy outline around her vision disappeared and the woman's eyes focused on the Huntress standing in the doorway.

"There you are. Now, what are you doing sneaking around in my restaurant after hours?"

Quinn searched for an answer and didn't get one out fast enough.

"Come on, girl. I don't have all night. These books won't balance themselves."

Quinn glanced at the pile of papers on the desk beside Inez and cleared her throat. "I'm Quinn, the Huntress from the clan here in Baltimore. You already know I work with Clark. I learned some things about the disappearances of your people and came to see if I could find out anything else."

"I don't know what you mean. Ain't nobody missing that I know of."

"That's not what your men upstairs said while they were cleaning up."

"Well, they talk too much," Inez said, annoyance in her tone. "I wouldn't put much stock in anything they say."

"Look, I'm not here to cause trouble, but if you have something going on, maybe with a certain Fae princess, I'm sure I can offer you some help."

At the mention of the princess, Inez's eyebrows lowered for an instant. Quinn swore it was a look of concern. It told Quinn she was on the right track.

"Filippa has gotten in my way, too, Inez. I'm sure you've heard some of it through the local gossips."

Inez smiled. "I have at that. You've proved to be a bit of a thorn in that stuck-up woman's side, from what I can tell. That doesn't mean I need your help with anything right now. Tell Clark I can handle my Fae problems in-house."

Quinn thought back to the encounter she'd witnessed with Avery in the parking lot a few days before. "What about your run-in with the other Huntress? At least I'm on your side. She's doing Filippa's bidding, and I know she threatened you. I'm surprised you're letting her get away with it. I thought badgers were tough."

Inez shifted halfway to badger form in an instant, jumping to her feet. The bared fangs and ripping snarl told Quinn she'd gone too far.

Holding up her hands, Quinn said, "I meant no offense. I came to help you, that's all."

"Didn't ask for help. Don't need help. The only reason I didn't rip that other girl's guts open is I can tell she's mixed up in something beyond her understanding. That one's an innocent, dangerous but not evil. Once I realized that I gave her a pass, kind of like I'm doing for you right now."

That described Avery for sure, though Quinn didn't like being lumped into the same category. She nodded, saying, "I've met her. That's an apt description of her. She's very capable as a fighter, though. Don't underestimate what she can do."

Inez shifted back to her human form but didn't sit down. She stared up at Quinn. "And you're here to do what? What can you do for me that I can't do for myself?"

"For one thing, I can find out what that poser Huntress is up to here in our town. She's staying with my clan, so I can keep an eye on her. It would be nice if you and I could work together and sort out what she and Gemma are doing here."

"I know what she wants, girl. The Fae have been after it for years ever since it disappeared about a hundred and fifty years ago."

"What? What are they after?"

Inez smiled. "The crystal well. It's been rumored to be buried here somewhere under the city for years. Many have studied archives and dug to look for it, but no one has found it."

"What is it?"

"No one knows, at least no one around here. Filippa might, but she's not telling anyone. All she wants is to find it. She came to me, looking for miners to work for her on a secret project. When I told her we didn't do that sort of work anymore, she didn't accept my concern that working under a modern city like this would be too dangerous. As soon as I said no, my people started getting snatched off the streets late at night."

"So, Clark was right," Quinn mused. "How many are missing?"

"Eighteen at the last count. I've gotten assurances they're alive and somewhere under the city. I just don't know where. Until I can find out, there's nothing I can do without risking their necks, which I will not do."

Quinn nodded. A glimmer of a plan started forming in her mind. "I think I can help you with that. I can find their location, so no one traces it back to you."

"How're you gonna do that?"

"Gemma, Avery's mistress, thinks I'm a no-talent hack. It'll be easy for me to hide what I'm doing while sneaking around and spying on them. I can track down where your people are and then let you know so you can do whatever you think is best."

Inez considered that, then, "I don't like taking help, but if you're gonna snoop anyway, I don't see no harm in it. If you find my people, I'd be obliged to you. We might have been good at digging in the mines at one time, but in the modern world, we don't have to be dirt scrabblers anymore. We want to work out in the sunshine like respectable folk."

"I understand that completely. I will keep your confidence. I won't even tell Clark unless it's absolutely necessary. We'll take care of this mess."

Inez nodded. She waved a hand in the air as she turned back to her bookkeeping. "Good, now git, and make sure you hide again. I don't want anyone knowing I met with you."

Quinn nodded and turned to leave. She whispered "mist" and faded from view as she climbed back up the stairs. She wasn't sure how she was going to track Filippa's hidden operation to find the crystal well. First thing, though, she had to find a way to get Avery to trust her more. Then the other girl might lead her to wherever Filippa had hidden the miners.

Arriving back at the parking lot, Quinn walked to the rear of the area before tapping her earpiece and calling Taylor.

"T, I'm ready to come back now."

"What did you find out?"

"Not too much," Quinn replied, hiding her conversation with Inez. "I think there's something going on, but we're going to have to come at it a different way."

Quinn was about to ask Taylor to hit the recall signal when a dozen motorcycles rode around from the front of the restaurant and pulled up by the rear kitchen entrance. The leader, riding a bike with a sidecar, pointed at the back entrance and shouted something.

"Ready to come back, Quinn?" Taylor asked.

"Hold up, T. Something's going on."

"What's up?"

Quinn shook her head. "Trouble, I think. I'll contact you again when I'm ready to come out of VR." She tapped the earpiece to shut down the connection. She hadn't shut off her hiding ability, so she was pretty sure the bikers hadn't spotted her.

At first, she thought maybe they were members of the

werebadger clan, but as she crossed the parking lot, she realized all of them were too tall. She caught a whiff of wet fur. They were some sort of shifter, but she didn't know what kind.

A few of the bikers dismounted and entered the kitchen, and people started shouting. Then one of the bikers stumbled back into the parking lot, clutching his face, blood flowing from between his fingers. Whoever they were after was fighting back.

More shouts and snarling came from inside and three more of the bikers went in, shifting form as they did. Their heads and features took on a feline shape, some with black fur, others with yellow-brown. Quinn guessed they were some sort of werepanther.

The one who sat on the lead bike pointed at the door and screamed, "Get me that old woman. Kill the others. It's time we sent them a message from the boss."

Realizing what was happening, Quinn didn't stop to think. She leaped into action. Drawing her Bowie, Quinn charged, angling to one side to catch the nearest of the bikers from behind.

She picked up speed and hit the werepanther, tucking her shoulder as she collided with him.

He grunted and pitched off his motorcycle, trying to twist to the side and reach for Quinn as he fell.

She rode him to the ground, driving her Bowie into his back in three quick thrusts. The last one struck home in his heart, the magical silver alloy blade smoking in the wound.

Quinn didn't stop to double-check her work. The remaining six shifters heard their comrade call out before he died. They let out low growls as they faced the attacker.

Knowing speed was her friend, Quinn dialed up her stamina bar and drew off some energy to juice up her quickness and strength. She'd hoped to take down more than one before the others recovered from the surprise attack. She hadn't counted on how tough the one she'd attacked first had been, or how many strikes it had taken to kill him.

As the six shifters fanned out in a semicircle to face her, Quinn feinted to the left, then charged to the right.

It worked. The werepanther on that side either didn't expect her speed boost or fell for the feint. It didn't matter which.

Dropping into a slide, Quinn passed between the biker's legs. She stabbed up into his abdomen and again into his groin as she went through.

She dug in with the heels of her boots, bounced to her feet behind him, and spun around. The shifter had doubled over, clutching both his crotch and belly. Even if he survived, he was out of this fight.

Quinn had to shift into defensive mode as the closest two closed in. One carried a baseball bat with spikes jutting from the end, and the other attacked with his panther claws.

She managed to fend off the first swing of the bat, but only by moving into the range of his comrade. Claws raked down her right shoulder, tearing into the leather jacket and ripping the skin below.

Quinn hissed in pain while she jumped back and to the side to avoid the follow-up blow from the other hand. She managed to score a glancing slash with her knife that caused the werepanther to yowl in pain and step back.

Unfortunately, another was ready to step into his spot, and the second moved around to swing at her again. She shifted left, barely ducking in time to avoid the spiked bat coming at her head.

She punched the thigh of the bat-wielder and got in a lucky strike when he was a second too late pulling his leg back. It wasn't much of a slash, though, not enough to do more than slow him down a little.

It would have to be enough because there were still four werepanthers facing her. The final one raised his arm, and Quinn realized too late he held a hand crossbow.

He fired, and the six-inch bolt flew at her before she could block or dodge it. The thick-shafted arrow punched into her already injured shoulder with enough force to knock her back.

Quinn stumbled and used the momentum to keep spinning while she put some distance between her and her attackers. As she did, she reassessed the situation.

At this point, it was obvious she couldn't take the remaining five, even with a few of them injured. Her right arm was toast for the time being, and she knew they wouldn't give her enough time to try to pull ley-line energy in to heal herself.

The shifters all had wild grins on their catlike faces, fangs showing. They'd fanned out to try to keep her from running. Soon she'd have no chance to escape.

Making the only move she had left, Quinn pulled up her HUD and said, "Mist."

She wasn't sure it would work the way she wanted, since every other time, no one had been watching her when she ducked into the shadows.

As soon as the haze appeared around her vision, Quinn dodged to the left, aiming for the gap between two of the shifters.

One of the ones behind her growled, "Where'd she go?"

"There," the one closest to her called, pointing in her direction. "I can still sort of see her."

Quinn angled away from that one and sprinted between two others. She drew on more stamina while she ran to gain both speed and stealth.

One of the two she went past must have seen something because he reached in her direction. Only by twisting at the last instant did she avoid contact, which would have broken the illusion.

As soon as she was outside the circle, she headed for the rear of the lot and the cover of the trees and bushes there. Behind her, the shifters twisted and looked in all directions, trying to find her.

A shout from the leader, who was still astride the bike with the sidecar, drew their attention. "Don't bother with the girl, get back over here."

Two of the werepanthers who'd gone inside the restaurant, came out holding a struggling Inez between them. She had been tied up, with her arms to her sides and her mouth gagged.

The leader pointed at his sidecar, and they dumped her in headfirst. He revved his engine, and his rear tire spat out gravel as he turned in the lot and aimed for the street.

The others, less the one Quinn had killed, helped their injured comrades onto their bikes and followed the leader onto the street. Soon Quinn stood alone in the lot. A flicker of fire caught her eye from inside the kitchen, then a fireball exploded through the restaurant's roof as the gas line inside ignited.

The blast knocked her down, even as far away as she was. Groaning as she climbed to her feet, Quinn tapped her earpiece. She had to get back. Clark needed to know about this and what she'd learned from Inez before the woman was taken.

"T, I need to come back. Call Clark, too."

"What's up? Your pattern in the system spiked a second ago."

"I'll tell you when I get there. I'm going to need to be patched up, too."

"Gotcha, get ready, I'm hitting the recall now."

The tugging pulled Quinn backward, and she dipped into the blackness.

CHAPTER THIRTEEN

Quinn opened her eyes and stared at the ceiling above her. She rolled over to sit up, cradling her right arm as she did.

"Damn, Quinn, that looks bad. Should we get you to the hospital or something?"

Quinn shook her head. "I can handle it. I just need to get up to my room and draw some energy from the ley lines nearby." She looked at the bolt embedded in her shoulder and gripped the shaft.

Miranda and Taylor both shouted, "No!"

Quinn ignored them and pulled at the embedded quarrel, twisting as she shouted through the pain. It came free, leaving an open wound that bled freely.

Taylor handed Quinn a wadded-up hand towel she grabbed from the table nearby. Quinn pressed it against the wound, pushing hard to staunch the flow of blood.

Miranda floated over and leaned in to look. "Those claw wounds look deep too, Quinn. What did you fight this time?"

Quinn started to shrug and winced as pain lanced through her shoulder. "I think they were werepanthers? Not sure, but that's what they looked like to me."

"You have to be careful with them, Quinn. They are usually ruthless and cruel, especially if they have a leader who can pull them into a group. They're usually loners or move in small family units. How many were there?"

"A dozen or so," Quinn replied. She stood up and tested her balance while leaning against the table for a few seconds. "They were part of a biker gang. When they attacked the werebadgers in the restaurant, I thought I could catch them by surprise. They were tougher than I expected, though. I only managed to cut one down before the others converged on me."

Taylor's eyes got wide. "All twelve of them?"

"Only six. The others were inside, killing the restaurant workers and kidnapping Inez. Six were bad enough. I only just escaped. I was lucky."

"Yes, you were," Clark said from the door.

Quinn glanced at him. "At least I tried to stop them."

"You weren't supposed to go back there. I told you I'd deal with it. I promised Inez."

"Well," Quinn replied, "Inez has been taken and the restaurant is toast, so I guess we're lucky I went out tonight. If I hadn't, I never would have found out what Gemma and Avery are up to here."

Clark shook his head. "They took Inez?"

Quinn nodded and explained the conversation she'd had with the woman and the subsequent events in the parking lot. "If I hadn't been there, we'd have no idea where she is."

"We still don't," Clark said. "There aren't any werepanthers in this area that I know of, so I'm not sure where they're hanging out."

"Won't the other supernaturals in town know something?" the Huntress asked. "I think they'd notice a gang of crazy werepanther bikers."

Clark said, "Werepanther gangs like that are kind of like the Columbian cartels of the shifter world. They are known to be bloodthirsty and hard on anyone who crosses them. If they're here in Baltimore, it'll be hard to root them out."

Clark touched Quinn's injured arm. "Do you need that looked at?"

"No," Quinn said, jerking her arm back. She groaned at the sudden movement. "I can handle it. Huntress genes, remember?"

"I know that, but you still have to stop the bleeding, or you'll leave a trail to your room. O'Malley will make you come back down and clean it up."

Taylor giggled, and Quinn glared at her. Her friend hid her smile behind her hand, but Quinn could still see it.

"I'm going upstairs. I'll be fine after I heal overnight. I'll see you all at breakfast."

Quinn headed for the door, sliding past Clark and out into the hall. She walked back to the bar entrance. It was late on a weeknight, so she didn't expect much of a crowd.

She was right; the place was nearly empty. Turning so her bloody shoulder was hidden from the patrons, Quinn rushed past the bar.

"I wondered if that was you," Gemma said as Quinn passed her.

Stopping, Quinn spotted the woman seated on a bar stool, sipping a glass of red wine.

"What?"

"Some friends of mine ran into some trouble tonight, and the girl they described sounded familiar. You should be careful. They think you owe them a blood debt now. You shouldn't have killed a member of the pride."

How did she know? Quinn tried to come up with a snappy retort, but her pain and exhaustion distracted her. All she said was, "Tell them to bring it."

Gemma smiled, "Oh, my dear, I don't have to tell them anything. They'll 'bring it' as you say all on their own. You've opened a can of worms by sticking your nose into business in which you have no part."

"This is my city, and I'm the clan's Huntress. If it happens here, it's my business."

"Not for much longer. I think my Avery will prove her point soon enough, and you'll be without a clan. There can only be one Huntress, you know."

"I'm not scared of you or Avery. She has some tricks, but she's not as great as you think she is. It's like you raised her in a convent. She has no idea what the real world is like."

Gemma smiled and sipped her wine but didn't answer.

"Wait, that's what you want, isn't it? You want someone you have control over so you can run things from the shadows."

"What's wrong with that? That's what Clark's trying to do, right?"

Quinn bristled. "Clark doesn't run me. He trains me and helps me learn things when I need them, but I'm the one who's in charge when it comes down to it. I'm the one who has to save everyone when things fall apart. You should be careful. Avery will eventually figure out what you're doing."

"You are adorable. I can see why he and Naomi keep you around. As for Avery, if she doesn't work out, there are others who can fill the role." Gemma pointed at her arm, dripping blood on the floor at her feet. "You should get that looked at. Avery is upstairs, I think. She might even try some healing magic on it if you ask nicely."

"I'm fine. I'll do it myself." Quinn stepped over the puddle of blood and started toward the apartment. If she stayed here, she was going to blurt out something she didn't want to say in front of Gemma.

She made it to the stairs without anyone else in O'Malley's noticing her injury. By the time she got to the second floor, Quinn had to stop at the top of the stairs to catch her breath. She realized she'd probably lost a lot more blood than she'd thought.

Quinn reached out to try to pull on the ley line junction running underground nearby, but when she tried to draw on it, she failed. The flow of energy bowed in her direction but snapped back as she lost hold of it. She was too tired, too drained to make it work.

Maybe if she got some sleep, she could energize from the ley line in the morning. Trudging to her apartment door, Quinn turned the key in the lock and pushed it open.

"Oh, my God, Quinn," Avery exclaimed as the Huntress entered. "What happened to you?"

"Don't act like you don't know. Gemma was just gloating about it downstairs."

"I don't know what you're talking about. I've been up here enjoying your bathtub for the last half-hour, and I was watching the telly before that. What did you do, stick your arm in a blender?"

Avery got up from the couch and came over to where Quinn stood in the tiny kitchen. She lifted Quinn's arm to study the injuries. The towel Quinn had been using to staunch the bleeding wound had become soaked.

Avery pulled it away, dropping it in the sink. She examined the wound, then grabbed a nearby tea towel from the drawer by the stove and pressed it against the still-oozing puncture.

Quinn tried to get away from the other woman's ministrations but had no strength left to resist. When Avery directed her to sit by the table with a gentle tug, she complied.

"Press this fresh towel against your shoulder while I help you get this jacket off." Avery's hands moved quickly but were gentle, surprising Quinn. When they'd come into physical contact recently, it had always been during training bouts, and maximum injury had been the goal. Now, though, she acted like she cared.

"You don't have to do this. I just need to go lie down and get some rest. I have a way of healing on my own."

"Nonsense," Avery said. "I just need to get a good look at your injuries, then I can do some healing. It's part of the skill set for a Huntress, right?"

"Uh, yeah, right. Um, okay, sure," Quinn stammered. "Go for it if that's what you want to do."

"You don't know what I'm talking about, do you? You can't lay on hands, can you?"

Quinn shook her head. "I don't know what that is, but I'm sure I can manage on my own."

As she said it, a wave of lightheadedness washed over her, and she struggled to stay upright in the chair. Quinn rested her good arm on the table for support. Despite that, she still swayed in her seat.

Avery finished wiping at the gashes from the panther claws and put down the cloth she'd been using. "Hold still. I have to connect with you to do this."

A tickle at the back of Quinn's consciousness expanded into an awareness that she wasn't alone in her head anymore.

"*Quinn, relax. It's just me,*" Avery's voice said in her mind. "*This is the Hunters' Mind Touch. Hunters have used it for millennia to communicate over short distances during hunts when stealth was imperative.*"

"*How? Clark never—*"

"*Not all Hunters possessed the skill. You definitely have it. I knew it from the first time I met you. Have you never communicated with anyone via your thoughts before?*"

Quinn thought back to the motherly voice she'd heard on occasion or the way she'd talked with the fallen clan leaders in the ceremonial chamber. Maybe this explained it.

"*I guess I have, sort of. I never knew what it was.*"

Avery's pleased amusement translated through the connection. "*Well, good. Now that we've connected, I can help you draw energy while I supplement with my own to heal your wounds.*"

"*I don't think I have the strength to do much right now,*" Quinn sent over the link.

"That's all right. I'll provide most of it. Here, let me show you how." Avery laid her bare hand over the crossbow wound and said, *"You might feel a little heat while I do this."*

"Do what?" Quinn started to ask out loud. She stopped as a searing pain shot through her arm. It ended as quickly as it started, leaving behind a pleasant warmth that spread into the rest of her body from her shoulder.

"All done," Avery said, taking her hand away. She went to the kitchen sink and started washing her hands.

Quinn checked her shoulder. The bloody puncture wound and the gouges from the claws had disappeared, replaced by faint white scars across her tanned skin. Quinn traced her fingers across the lines.

Avery came back with a huge smile on her face. "All better, right?"

"Yes," Quinn said. "Thank you."

"Not a problem. We Huntress gals have to stick together. You'd do the same for me, after all."

Quinn nodded. She probably would, despite their rivalry.

"What was that you said when you told me I knew what had happened to you?" Avery asked. "You said Gemma was involved?"

"You don't have to pretend, Avery," Quinn said, trying not to be annoyed at the woman who'd just healed her. "You already told me about your connection to Filippa."

Confusion clouded Avery's expression. "What does the Fae princess have to do with this? She was our benefactor and helped protect us immediately after the purges."

Quinn grew annoyed. "Do I have to spell it out for you? Avery, Gemma brought you here to help her search for a hidden artifact. Something valuable Filippa wants. You have to know about it. You were there days ago in the parking lot. You threatened Inez. I saw you."

Avery stared at Quinn, trying to process what she'd said. "You're referring to the werebadger woman?"

Quinn nodded.

"Gemma told me to confront the woman because of a family contract they had with her. That's all. The woman owed us something, and I was there to make sure she fulfilled her end of the bargain."

Quinn stared at Avery, trying to discern if she was lying.

Avery pointed at Quinn. "What were you doing there? Why were you spying on me?"

"I didn't even know who you were then. Clark and I had been investigating some suspicious disappearances in the city. It linked back to Inez and the werebadgers. We went there to locate them and bring them back to their families. Whatever you did when you threatened her made her shut up. She wouldn't tell us anything."

"I don't understand what that has to do with your injuries tonight?" Avery asked. "I've only been there the one time. I haven't been back since. As far as I know, Gemma got what she wanted."

"And what was that?" Quinn asked. "What is it that Gemma wants bad enough to kill innocent shifters in my town and burn down their homes and businesses?"

"That makes no sense. What proof do you have Gemma was involved?"

Quinn pointed at her shoulder. "This happened at the

restaurant tonight. Gemma had a pack of werepanthers show up—"

"It's a pride," Avery interrupted.

"What?"

"A group of werepanthers or any cat shifters are called prides, like with lions in the wild."

"Stop that. It's annoying."

"What? I was only—"

Quinn held up a hand, silencing Avery. "Always correcting me and showing me how much you know about everything supernatural. I get it. I didn't grow up studying all this stuff every minute of every day. I don't need you rubbing my nose in it all the time."

"Fine, I'll try. Now tell me about the werepanthers. You think Gemma had something to do with their attack on the werebadgers?"

"I'm sure of it, just like I'm sure Filippa is ultimately behind all this as part of some twisted plan to bring her own version of the Huntress prophecy to life."

"Quinn, I'm not saying Gemma is a perfect person. She can be very harsh when she wants to be. I know because I've lived with her nearly all my life. That doesn't mean she's capable of something like this. What you describe is evil. She could never hide something like that from me. I grew up learning that we Hunters protect the helpless, save the innocent, and fight evil in all its forms."

Something Avery said triggered a random thought in Quinn. "You've trained to fight them, but you've never actually fought one, have you?"

"A supernatural like a shifter?" Avery asked in reply. She shook her head, and her face turned almost the color of her hair. "No. Facing down the werebadger leader was my first real encounter outside of training."

Suddenly a lot of things shifted into place for Quinn. Avery had many skills, but she'd never proven herself in real combat. Quinn had on numerous occasions. Was Avery nothing more than a pawn being used by Gemma to accomplish some part of Filippa's grand plan?

Avery said, "I assure you I would handle myself quite well in actual combat. All my instructors have given me the highest marks."

"High marks aren't everything. Neither is strength. There's something you learn on the streets, something an old homeless vet once called 'grit.' He told me I had it. When I asked what it was, he said grit is the thing that pushes you forward when you can't keep going. Until you've been in combat and found out how much grit you have, you can't know what you'll do."

"I don't go out looking for fights, Quinn. That's not what we're supposed to do."

"I guess we'll just have to wait and see, then," Quinn said. "Look, I've had a hard day and evening. I want to go shower and get some rest. For what it's worth, I believe you. I don't know what Gemma's up to, and I don't think you know either."

Avery nodded. "Thank you. I'm sure you're mistaken about her, but if she's done something untoward in some way, I'll tell you. As I said before, we Huntresses have to stick together."

Quinn smiled and turned toward her bedroom. "G'night," she called as she shut the door.

A muffled reply from Avery filtered through from the

other room, and Quinn walked over and flopped onto the bed, rolling onto her back to stare at the ceiling.

Something vibrated against her side and she glanced down, startled at first until she saw the dragon egg pressed against her.

"Oh, hi, you. I suppose you heard all that?"

Buzzz buzzz.

"Should I believe her?

Buzzz buzzz.

Quinn looked at the pattern of water stains on the ceiling. "I don't know. I want to believe her. She seems so sincere, even in the midst of her annoying way of getting everything so right all the time. But maybe she's deceiving me."

Buzzz.

"Fine, just because she's better at some stuff isn't a reason not to believe her. She's never lied to me that I can tell, after all."

Quinn yawned and shook her head. "Whatever she did to heal me, it left me tired. Maybe I'll skip…the shower…"

As she dozed off, the dragon egg rolled around and nestled against the curve of Quinn's neck and shoulder, buzzing gently in time with her slow, steady breaths.

CHAPTER FOURTEEN

Quinn sat up with a start, staring around her room in the darkness. Someone had called her name, someone familiar. Sliding off the bed, she walked barefoot across the floor to the bedroom door, opening it quietly and peeking out to check on Avery.

The other Huntress snored lightly on the sofa, deep in sleep. Quinn stared at her for a few seconds, trying to decide if the girl was faking it and had been messing with her.

Avery continued to lie there, unmoving. Quinn tiptoed out past her to check the apartment door. It was locked. No one was outside when she peered through the peephole.

She was about to head back to her room when a glint on the floor caught her eye. A sparkling line started just inside the apartment and disappeared beneath the door to the hallway outside. She looked through the peephole again. Still nobody there.

Ignoring her bare feet, Quinn opened the door and checked the hallway outside.

Yep, empty.

The glittering gold trail began at her doorway and went down the hallway to the stairs. Checking to make sure Avery was still asleep, Quinn pulled the door shut behind her and followed it.

Reaching the end of the hall, the trail turned onto the staircase. Instead of going down, it led up to the third floor.

Without hesitating, Quinn climbed the stairs and followed the narrow hallway until she stood with Taylor's apartment door on one side and the metal ladder leading up to the roof on the other.

She looked down. The trail ended here. Quinn considered knocking on her friend's door and waking her up. Maybe she'd be able to detect any magic in use.

Quinn stood with her hand raised to rap on the door, stopping as the distant voice once again called her name. There was something oddly familiar about it, but she couldn't say who it was. She looked up the ladder to the roof. The voice had come from there.

After climbing the ladder and unlocking the latch holding the hatch cover closed, Quinn swung her legs over. The tar on the flat roof warmed her bare feet after absorbing the sunlight all day. It was a pleasant feeling in the chilly night air.

The thin gold trail continued to the low parapet that extended up from the building's walls on three sides of the slightly sloped roof. At the end of the trail, nestled against the red bricks, was the dragon egg.

Quinn scooped it up. "What are you doing up here? How did you even…"

The egg vibrated in Quinn's arms, cutting her off. At the same instant, a sparkling flash in the corner of her eye distracted her. It took a few seconds for Quinn to realize where it came from.

Activating her HUD, the sparkle she couldn't quite see was replaced by a new icon—a short, stubby arrow with a point at one end and three angled lines at the base to signify fletching. When she concentrated on it, the word "scout" appeared for a few seconds before fading.

Quinn clicked the scout icon and a transparent map of the city overlaid her view of the downtown skyline. Quinn studied the map, trying to find whatever the egg wanted her to see.

One area was shaded in pale yellow as if someone had highlighted it. She focused on it, and the map zoomed in until she hovered over the Federal Hill neighborhood by the harbor. Quinn tried to make out what it was about the area she was supposed to notice, but nothing leaped out at her. It looked just like every other part of the city, other than the yellow shading.

Quinn looked down at the egg cradled in her arms. It shook violently, and she fumbled to get a better grip. It slipped from her grasp, and Quinn shouted as she dove to catch it before it fell to the ground far below. Then she fell too, the ground racing up at her, the egg just beyond the reach of her fingers.

Gasping for breath, Quinn's eyes opened as her hands flailed at the covers on her bed. A faint purring vibration against her neck drew her attention to the egg nestled there.

Rolling to her side, Quinn stroked the shell. "What are you up to, you little booger? What's on that hill you want me to see?"

The egg didn't respond, just continued the steady, rhythmic vibration she'd come to associate with sleep. Had she shared a dream with the tiny dragon inside, or was there something more to see?

Quinn didn't know the answer, and the egg wasn't talking. She thought about it until her eyes grew heavy again; she was still tired from the fight and healing earlier. Giving in at last, she drifted back to sleep.

CHAPTER FIFTEEN

The next morning, Quinn rose early and snuck past Avery. The girl was still snoring on the couch, much as she had in the dream the night before. After going down to the bar, she dug around in the kitchen, searching for something to eat. She eventually made herself some toast and smeared peanut butter on it.

Quinn poured herself a glass of milk and carried the glass and plate back out to the club, where she sat at the bar in the near darkness. She'd finished half the peanut butter toast when the overhead lights switched on, and she spun around to see who'd arrived.

Quinn relaxed when she spotted Juni.

"Hey, Quinn. You're up early. I saw you last night, heading up to your room. You looked done in." The leprechaun girl tilted her head to the side and glanced at Quinn's right arm. "That shoulder better now? You were bleeding pretty bad."

Quinn brought her left hand up and rubbed her

shoulder self-consciously. "It's better now, thank you. Sorry if I left you a mess to clean up."

"We took care of it. It's not the first time we've had blood on the floor in here, believe me."

Quinn smiled and went back to her toast and milk while Juni switched on the rest of the lights, leaving the bar area until last. Juni walked behind the tall countertop, stepping onto the raised floor built to accommodate the owner, his daughter, and the other leprechaun workers.

As Quinn ate, Juni prepped the bar for the day's patrons. The Huntress noticed something she'd never spotted before: a small framed image about the size of a sheet of standard notebook paper hung in the center of the oval bar area. Yellowed with age, it looked like an old map of the city.

"Juni, can I take a look at that picture?"

The waitress looked where Quinn pointed. "This old thing? It's from an antique pamphlet my dad found. He said he liked the map because it showed the city when things were simpler here in Baltimore."

"What did he mean by that?" Quinn asked.

Juni rolled her eyes. "I have no idea. Here, you can take a look closer if you want." She handed the paper map in its brown wooden frame to Quinn and returned to her work setting up the bar for the day.

Quinn studied the paper. The lines had faded, but she could make out most of the details. Some areas of the city were highlighted with expanded views. One of them was the area around Federal Hill. It was the heading at the top of the expanded section that caught her eye.

The Crystal Caves and Old Silica Mines

"Juni, when did this old map come from?"

"Daddy said it was when he and mother first met, so that would make it sometime in the late 1800s after the Civil War. Why?"

"It shows things I've never heard of before, and I've lived in the city all my life."

"Like what?"

The tiny woman stopped what she was doing and came over.

Quinn pointed at the Federal Hill area. "These caves. I never knew there were caves beneath Federal Hill?"

"Oh, sure. Those tunnels are one of the oldest legends of the city. They've been filled in for years, though. The city had it done after parts of the hill collapsed from a cave-in and threatened some of the homes on the hill above."

Quinn's hopes sank. "All of them?"

"As far as I know. They were pretty dangerous. People used to get stuck or trapped down there all the time. I guess the city finally got tired of rescuing them. Nothing left of it as far as I know."

Juni went back to setting up, leaving the back of the bar, going around taking chairs down from atop the tables, and arranging them for the lunch crowd coming in a few hours.

Quinn took a bite of her toast and stared at the old pamphlet. She looked over her shoulder to make sure Juni was busy and then flipped the frame over, sliding out the cardboard insert until she could reach the paper inside. It was so fragile it started to tear as she tried to fold it. Working as fast as she dared with the fragile paper, she slipped it into the pocket of the hooded sweatshirt she wore.

After checking on Juni again, Quinn pushed the cardboard back into place, reached over the bar top, and pushed the frame behind the cash register. No one would notice it in the shadows there.

Quinn popped the final piece of toast into her mouth, then picked up her empty plate and glass and headed for the kitchen. "I'll put these in the dishwasher tray for you, Juni. Thanks for breakfast."

"No problem, Quinn. Take care today. I think Clark has something special planned for you and Avery."

"What's that? Tell me what you heard."

Juni shook her head. "I don't know any details. Sorry. I just saw Clark, Naomi, and Gemma with their heads together last night. I figured they must be cooking up something for this contest they have going between the two of you."

"I better go up and check on Avery, then. She'll want to get something to eat before they call us down."

Quinn dropped off the plate and glass in the kitchen, then went to her apartment. When she opened the door, she heard Avery humming in the living room. She had a pleasant voice, although Quinn didn't know the tune. It had a haunting quality and made her sort of sad.

Avery looked up when Quinn walked in, ceasing her humming.

"Don't stop singing on my account," the Huntress said. "I kind of liked it. What's the name of that song?"

Avery blushed. "It's not one you'd know. It's a funeral dirge that used to be sung by the clans over the graves of members killed on a hunt. I think it has its roots in an ancient Germanic folk song. I found a recording of it during my studies. I couldn't understand the words, but the tune stuck."

"I like it, too," Quinn said. "It's sad, but it's pretty. It's the kind of thing I might want sung at my funeral someday."

Avery smiled. "Me, too. It's peaceful, and it sort of sets my mind at ease. I could imagine hearing it as a ghost and letting it take me to the higher planes. Maybe we could play it for your friend Miranda so she can finally go where she belongs."

"Why does she need to go anywhere? Miranda belongs here with us. She's chosen to stay here and help us. She's part of the clan. She has a nickname and everything."

"What do you call her?" Avery asked.

"Well, it's just something Taylor and I came up with. We call her our 'spectral godmother' sometimes. To be honest, we mostly use it when she's hovering over us too much."

"Hovering," Avery said, laughing. "I get it."

Quinn smiled at the joke she'd missed as she said it. "Uh, yeah, anyway, she belongs here with us. She's been a lot of help to Taylor with the witch side of being our tech witch."

"What's your nickname?" Avery asked.

"I'm the Huntress, I guess. That's all." She shrugged.

"We'll have to find you a new one since I'll be taking that particular title after the bout coming up."

Quinn bit back a sharp reply, focusing on the second half of the other girl's response. It surprised her. "What are you talking about? I only just found out we had something planned for later. How did you know?"

"Gemma mentioned it to me when I came up to the apartment last night. She told me to tell you about it, but I forgot when I had to heal your arm. How's it feeling, by the way?"

Quinn rotated her arm at the shoulder and nodded. "It feels good as new. Thanks for that. I wish I knew how to do it. I can heal myself sometimes, but things have to be a certain way, I guess. It didn't work last night."

"You said that last night," Avery said. "I meant to ask you what you were talking about."

"It's ley lines. I can siphon power from them if there are any close by."

"You can? That has to be incredibly dangerous, handling all that power."

Quinn smiled. She finally had one up on Avery. "I don't know about dangerous, but it's certainly a rush when you do it. If I take in too much, my skin glows, and the light I give off can burn a vampire if I'm not careful."

"Wow, I'd love to see what you look like glowing. You're already beautiful. I can't imagine what that would look like, adding a magical glow."

It was Quinn's turn to blush, and she hid her smile at the compliment behind a fake cough. "Yeah, uh, thank you. Like I said last night, I could have found a way to do it myself, but it was nice to have you do it for me. Was it easy to learn?"

Avery rolled her eyes. "Ugh, it took me for*ever* to master it. Gemma was so cross with me. Honestly, I envy what you can do, Quinn. You can't use my sort of healing spell on yourself. It's all about channeling your Huntress energy outward to merge with another. It can't be turned around."

Quinn nodded. "I guess healing yourself is good, too."

"Did Clark teach your thing to you?" Avery asked.

"Oh, no, I learned by accident," Quinn replied. "Miranda and Clark were trying to teach me how magical energy worked and how to sense the ley lines. I reached out with my mind and bent one in my direction by accident. They were super-pissed at me."

"What did it feel like to have that sort of power coursing through you?" Avery had sat down on the sofa and leaned forward, intent on what Quinn was saying.

"Not comfortable, that's for sure. At the same time, though, part of it feels like when you…" Quinn's voice trailed off, and she rubbed her hand past the front of her hip.

Avery blushed a whole new shade of red at that reference, and Quinn laughed. She was getting a different view of her competition.

"Anyway, I've had to channel that kind of power three times, and each time, I've barely survived. I figure there are better ways to almost kill myself, no matter what a rush it is. I mean, no one wants to get struck by lightning four times."

The two of them chuckled together as they gathered their things to take down to the training room. Quinn was sorry to see the conversation end. Soon they'd be adversaries again, and this new closeness would go away. Quinn couldn't help but think that in a different time and place, she and Avery could be friends, or maybe even more.

Quinn took the folded map from the bar and placed it

in the top drawer of her dresser, then packed her workout bag. Once they'd each selected a spare outfit and grabbed a towel for the training room, she and Avery headed downstairs in search of Clark and Gemma. It was time to see what their elders had planned for the two of them.

CHAPTER SIXTEEN

Clark, Naomi, and Gemma waited for the two Huntresses in the training room. They stood at the center of the mats and were talking in hushed tones when Quinn and Avery arrived.

Naomi smiled at the two of them. "You seem chummy. Striking up a friendship with the enemy, Quinn?"

Avery shook her head. "Quinn is not my enemy, Naomi. She will become my most trusted lieutenant when the time comes for me to assume my place as the Huntress of legend."

Quinn shot Avery a sharp look. Just like that, their friendly chatter upstairs got flushed away.

"Speak for yourself, Avery. I'm nobody's lieutenant, trusted or otherwise."

Gemma laughed. "Good, Quinn. Maybe you can channel that anger into something resembling a decent defense in today's match."

Quinn growled deep in her throat and opened her mouth to reply.

Clark stepped forward and interrupted her. "Why don't I explain the rules for today's contest to the ladies?"

"Good idea," Naomi said. "It wouldn't do for them to off each other right here when they've got other things to do."

Quinn didn't like where this was going. "What do you have up your sleeve, Clark?"

"Gemma and I think you two have done enough in the confines of the Hunter complex. It's time to apply what you've learned in a contest that pits your individual strengths against each other in the outside world."

Avery bounced on the balls of her feet. "What are we doing? Is there a real hunt this time?"

Gemma smiled, although Quinn noticed the smile didn't quite reach her eyes.

"Avery, dear, that sort of hunt is rare these days, but this will approximate it pretty well. Clark will take you and I will take Quinn out into the city. We will drop you off. After that, your task will be to track the other without their knowing it. Clark and I will trail you both in our vehicles and on foot when necessary. Once you're in a position where you could attack in a way that wouldn't alert the public around you to your presence, announce yourself, and the exercise is over."

Clark nodded. "Because Gemma and I will both be present when the winner announces their attack, we will judge if it would be successful."

"This is a winner-take-all event," Gemma said. "After this, there will only be one Huntress to fulfill the prophecy. We will know the other to be an untrained poser."

Quinn scowled but held her tongue. Responding wasn't going to solve anything. It was time for her to step up and show Avery how different things were in the real world.

"I'm ready," Quinn announced. "Let's get this over with."

"Very well," Gemma said. "You come with me. Clark will collect Avery, and we will begin."

Gemma left the training room. Quinn started to follow.

Naomi stopped with a hand on her shoulder. "Be careful, Quinn. Don't assume you've got any sort of advantage here. This is too important."

Quinn started to snap at her mother that she was fine, but she stopped. Instead, she gave Naomi a slight smile and nodded. She had to run to catch up to Gemma, who had not slowed her fast stride down the long hallway to O'Malley's.

When Quinn caught up with the other woman, Gemma said, "Do keep up, Quinn. It would be nice to give yourself a sporting chance before you lose."

Grinding her teeth together, she bit back a reply and followed the other woman to the alley where the supernatural bar's hidden entrance lay. Gemma pulled a car remote from her pocket and pointed it at a silver luxury sedan parked nearby.

"Get in. We have a little way to go."

"How far?" Quinn asked. "I don't want to be walking all day just to get back to the city."

"If I just drop you downtown, Avery will locate you in a few minutes," Gemma said. "No, for this to be a true test of everything I've taught her, I have to make it hard enough to mean something to Clark when she wins."

"*If* she wins."

"My dear, some might appreciate your persistence as

some sort of moxie. I'm not one of them. This is preordained. Someone predicted the outcome of today long before either of us was born."

"We'll see." Quinn reached under her coat and checked on her Bowie. She never went anywhere without it, even to the training room. Had they stayed, she would have swapped it out there. Now she was glad for her paranoid habit.

Gemma drove through the city, occasionally checking her phone's map app. She wasn't using route directions, so Quinn didn't know where she was going.

To her surprise, Gemma headed south to a location just outside of the beltway—the city's international airport. The woman pulled the sedan to a stop along a fence beside one of the runways.

"Get out."

"Here?" Quinn asked. "There's nothing around here. How am I supposed to get back to the city?"

"That's not my problem. I don't care if you sit down on the side of the road and wait for Avery to find you."

Quinn reached for the handle and opened the door. She hopped out, barely shutting the door before Gemma hit the gas and pulled away, merging into the busy airport traffic.

She looked around, making sure there wasn't any immediate danger. It would be just her luck that Clark and Gemma decided to go to the same place. That would end this game fast.

Once she was sure it was safe, Quinn took stock of what she had. That included the pocket of vending machine change she'd happened to scoop off her dresser that morning. She also had a city transit pass, which she realized was about to come in really handy.

Mind made up, Quinn pulled up her HUD and activated her map while she clicked on the triangular tracking icon. She remembered the newly acquired scout icon, so she clicked that as well.

The map didn't show Avery at first, and Quinn tried different things to find her. She needed some sort of connection to the other girl, and she remembered the healing spell from the night before. She laid her left hand across her right shoulder and thought about the connection Avery's spell might have created. Quinn wasn't sure it would work, but it was all she had.

As soon as she closed her eyes and concentrated, an icon of a katana sword appeared on the map display. Clark had taken Avery downtown and dropped her near the baseball and football stadiums. Right now, Avery was walking somewhere near the outfield in Oriole Park at Camden Yards.

That solved one problem. She pulled out her MTA pass and started walking toward the airport train station. It would take her right to the stadium complex downtown.

As she walked, Quinn whispered, "Mist." She waited for the hazy circle to appear around what she saw. She didn't know if it also obscured her from someone magically tracking her, but it was worth a try.

She got lucky and caught the next train just as it was leaving the station. The attendant at the turnstiles stared wide-eyed when she swiped her pass and walked through. She realized all he saw was the screen go green and the turnstile spin on its own.

Quinn smiled and steered in the guy's direction. She walked up behind him and said, "Ghost rider. Beware."

She moved away as the man spun, searching for the source of the voice. Quinn had to stifle her giggle as she ran between the last train car's closing doors and settled into a nearly empty seating area.

A quick check of the HUD' map showed Avery moving toward the harbor area near the stadiums. She wasn't coming in Quinn's direction, which puzzled her. Had her hiding skill worked or was Avery luring her into a trap?

Quinn knew she'd have to be ready for that eventuality. Avery had mad skills, and she was sure the other girl hadn't shown all she was capable of.

She used the twelve-minute jaunt between the airport and downtown to try to think of all the ways Avery could trip her up when Quinn finally tracked her down. There was much Quinn didn't know about the other girl, even after all their chats in the apartment.

Quinn knew she couldn't keep her hiding ability active forever. It would eventually run down, depleting the magical energy it ran on. It used to draw from her amulet, but when the pendant was destroyed, she'd somehow started to draw on something else, either within herself or from nearby magic. She had crafted her new amulet, but she rarely activated its protective magic since she now had mojo of her own.

As she rode, Quinn thought about that inner energy and brought up her stamina bar to see if she was drawing on that. When it showed a full hundred percent, another idea popped into her head. Could she use this hidden inner reserve to somehow supplement her stamina?

Focusing on the green bar in the HUD, Quinn concentrated on increasing its capacity. As she did, the haze around her vision indicating the shadow-hiding skill flickered, then went away. There was no one in the car with her, so nobody noticed her sudden appearance out of thin air.

Realizing she was onto something, Quinn drilled down. She narrowed her attention to the end of the stamina bar that would extend should she find a way to charge it. It took three tries before she figured out how she'd drawn power from her hiding skill.

Feeling the spare energy surging within her mind's grasp, Quinn stared at the hovering stamina bar. A gap appeared as the area it occupied expanded, and the green bar slowly grew to fill the added space. When it stopped expanding, Quinn let her focus slip away. The new, more powerful stamina bar remained filled.

Quinn had been so wrapped up in this new discovery, she barely noticed they had almost arrived at the stadium station.

As the train pulled into the platform, Quinn checked the area outside for any signs of a trap. Not seeing anything, she waited until the last instant, then jumped up, engaged her hiding skill again, and slipped through the closing doors. The others leaving the train had already started down to the street, so Quinn headed for the stairs, too. As she walked, she tried to predict the ways Avery might try to trick her.

That was important because she needed to come up with a counter-plan to foil whatever Avery had in mind, even if she didn't know what that was.

Once she was on the street, Quinn pulled up the HUD map overlay and searched for the other Huntress again. She'd been heading east toward the Inner Harbor's tourist area. The two pavilions there would be crowded at this time of day with shoppers and people heading to an early lunch in one of the restaurants. It would be easy for Avery to hide in the jumble of people. Quinn searched the HUD as she walked in that direction but couldn't find any sign of the other Huntress. It was like she'd disappeared. Maybe she'd realized Quinn was tracking her.

Quinn had almost reached the first of the two shopping pavilions by the water when a flicker in the HUD drew her attention. It was the arrow scout icon, and it flashed between yellow and red. She stopped and tried to activate it by mentally clicking on it.

Nothing happened.

She stood by the road, puzzled by the unknown notification when a chill ran down her spine and her amulet grew ice-cold against her chest, warning her like it used to.

Quinn spun around, expecting to find Avery standing there. The scent of wet fur told her she was wrong.

Bringing her hand down in a chopping motion, she acted on pure instinct. Her sudden reaction caught the assailant by surprise, and she blocked the knife coming at her back.

Shock registered on the man's face, and Quinn took advantage of it to grab his wrist and twist his arm up and out while squeezing as hard as she could. She drew upon her stamina automatically to increase her strength.

Bones ground together beneath her iron grip, and the

knife fell from the spasming fingers as she broke the shifter's wrist.

She jammed her other hand against the taller man's throat, driving him into a nearby light pole and tightening her grip until the guy's breaths came in painful wheezes.

"Who sent you? How did you find me?"

"N-no one," he croaked. "I just saw you walking and tried to pick your pocket."

Quinn squeezed the man's broken wrist harder. She drew a deep breath, trying to tag what kind of shifter he was by the distinctive scent. Quinn's eyes widened when she placed the smell.

Werepanther. He smelled just like the bikers from the other night.

"You're lying," she said as he groaned. "You were there the other night when you and your fellow goons snatched Inez. There's no way you showed up here by accident." Quinn pressed harder with the hand on the guy's throat.

A crowd had started to gather, and several people were on their phones. A few were recording the encounter. She realized her shadow hiding ability had canceled out when she turned to meet her attacker. It wasn't good to get this kind of attention.

Quinn knew who'd sent him, or suspected she did, anyway. She didn't have the time to do what she needed to do. The police would be here soon, and she didn't want to answer awkward questions about a dead body on the street or why she was walking around with a huge Bowie knife.

"Tell the one who sent you that I'm on to them. There will be a time of reckoning. Tell them the Huntress is coming."

She released both hands and took two steps back. The werepanther stared wide-eyed at the crowd that had gathered around them. He clutched the injured arm to his chest and pushed through the ring of bystanders, then ran across all four lanes of Pratt street. Cars screeched to a halt and horns blared, but he made it safely to the other side and disappeared between two buildings.

Quinn watched him go and then realized she had better disappear, too. She started to move into the crowd around her, shoving her way to the open space beyond them. Once she was free of contact, she could activate her hiding icon.

A hand clamped down on her shoulder.

Quinn spun around, reaching for her Bowie.

Her hand dropped to her side when she saw who it was.

Clark stood there disappointment plain in his expression. Just behind him stood Avery, a broad grin on her face. Gemma stood nearby too, oozing satisfaction.

Clark shook his head and turned to Gemma. "Looks like you win."

"No!" Quinn shouted. "That's not fair. I was just attacked by a shifter. Didn't you see him?"

"No, Quinn," Clark said. "I didn't. I was tailing Avery. She just raised her hand and pointed at this crowd of people. I didn't see you until you shouldered your way through them into the clear."

Quinn pointed at the lamppost. The crowd had mostly cleared, bystanders heading about their business. "The attack happened there. He tried to knife me. Come on. I'll show you the knife. It has to still be on the sidewalk over there."

"It doesn't matter," Clark said. "Avery spotted you first,

and she could've made the kill and gotten away without anyone seeing her. That gives her the win—the final win."

Gemma sauntered up to stand beside Clark. "That was even easier than I expected. Caught right out in the open like a common pedestrian."

Quinn's whole body trembled. Clenching her teeth, she said. "That was all part of your plan, wasn't it? Send one of your pet werepanthers to attack me and then wait for me to be distracted so Avery could get close enough to win."

Gemma placed raised her hand to her chest. "Quinn, dear, I don't know what you mean. I had nothing to do with this encounter you're talking about. Where is this cat shifter you speak of?"

"He ran off. I didn't want to kill him in front of a crowd of bystanders. Now I'm thinking I should have. Then I'd have the video to prove—"

"Prove what, exactly? Prove that you know how to kill? We know you can do that. The question is whether you have the skills needed to lead this little clan of yours."

Gemma turned to Clark. "I think this settles things once and for all. Avery is the Huntress. Your girl is the pretender. Why don't you two go back to O'Malley's and figure out how quickly you can move your stuff out. The Hunter chambers are mine now."

Clark's eyes darkened, but he said nothing. He gave a nodding jerk of his head and walked away. "Come on, Quinn. We need to get back."

Quinn shot one last glance at Gemma and Avery, then jogged after Clark. "Why are you giving in? They cheated. Gemma sent that guy after me on purpose."

"We'll talk about it when we get back to the bar." Clark

pointed at his beat-up sedan in the lot across the street. "Let's go. I need to figure out how to get us out of this mess while we drive back."

Quinn followed him across the street and climbed into the passenger seat. Clark got in and started the car. He didn't say another word to her all the way back to O'Malley's.

CHAPTER SEVENTEEN

Clark parked in the alley by the bar and got out, still without saying a word. He went down the stairs to the hidden basement entrance.

Quinn sighed. She needed to talk this out with him. Gemma was up to something. She must be close to finding the Crystal Well and had to get Quinn out of the way. She'd planned this whole contest with that in mind.

Now all Quinn could do was play catch up. She needed to find a way to stop the woman. If she let Gemma do this to her, she won the war without a fight. Today's loss was a single battle as far as Quinn was concerned. Avery had won most of the training contests, but Quinn knew deep down the other woman didn't have what it took to be the Huntress. She'd been too sheltered and had no idea what Gemma had hidden from her growing up.

Climbing out of the car and checking to make sure the door was locked, Quinn went down to the entrance, nodding at Jonas, the giant bouncer sitting on his stool just inside.

The big man chuckled as she entered. "What'd you do to piss off Clark this time, Quinn?"

Quinn started to snap back but saw the good-natured grin on his face and realized he didn't mean any harm. He had no part in what was going on.

Quinn shrugged. "Does he need a reason?"

Jonas laughed at that and shook his head as he waved her on through to the inner entrance.

Quinn walked right into the middle of the lunch rush. Many of the supernaturals from the surrounding community came here to eat on their midday breaks. Paddy's kitchen staff excelled at typical pub food, and they also provided quite a few special needs items for certain kinds of creatures. That was one of the reasons they'd chosen to make this their home base. Even Naomi could get food when needed.

Quinn spotted Taylor seated at their usual table right next to the bar. Naomi sat with her, and Miranda hovered there, too.

Taylor waved, seeing Quinn at the same time. "Quinn, come on over."

Quinn sat down in the open seat. She didn't feel like talking, so she picked up one of the menus from the slot beside the salt and pepper in the center of the table. She opened it and scanned the items, even though she wasn't all that hungry.

Naomi chuckled. "What did you do to put Clark in a mood? He acts like you lost the challenge."

Quinn glanced up, met her mother's eyes, and then looked back down at the menu.

"You didn't?" Naomi rolled her eyes. "Quinn, this was

your chance to show how you were different from Avery out in the field."

"I'm not stupid. I know that."

Taylor asked, "Then what happened? This should have been the best way for you to beat them."

"They cheated."

Naomi pressed her lips together. Quinn waited for her mother to yell at her. Instead, she seemed almost sad. "Of course they did. You were supposed to allow for that. This isn't your first time out there in real life, Quinn. You learned this lesson the hard way."

"Don't you think I know it? I was ready for trickery. I wasn't ready for a random attack by a werepanther who almost gutted me in the middle of a crowd at the Inner Harbor. I had to defend myself and deal with the attack. By the time I'd finished disarming him and running him off, Avery popped out and claimed the win. I didn't have a chance."

Taylor looked from Quinn to Naomi and back. "So, now what?"

"Now," Quinn said, "we stop Gemma from finding the Crystal Well."

Naomi shook her head. "What's this well?"

"I'm not sure. I only know Gemma came here to look for it. She's working with Filippa. If we can keep her from finding it, she'll go back to wherever she came from, and hopefully take Avery with her."

"What can we do to help?" Miranda asked.

"I need to go back into VR. I have a big advantage in there. First, though, I have to figure out where Gemma is hiding the werebadgers. I'm pretty sure she's using them to open up the old tunnels beneath Federal Hill. That's where she believes the artifact is located, and I think she's right. The only problem is we'd know it if she just started digging up the whole neighborhood. That means she has to have a way to conceal what she's doing."

"I can help with that," Taylor said. "If someone is using some sort of construction around there for cover, they'd have to apply to the city for permits. I can see what permits have been approved lately."

"Good," Quinn said. "Also, can you see if there's any connection in the area around Federal Hill related to an old silica mine and the tunnels associated with it? According to Juni, they were either filled in or caved in on their own over a hundred years ago. I think they have something to do with the Crystal Well."

Taylor nodded. "I'm on it. I'll start as soon as I get back. I need to finish this burger first."

"Go ahead and eat. I need something, too," Quinn said. "We'll all dive in and start looking as soon as we're finished."

It still amazed Quinn how hungry she got after using her abilities. There seemed to be a siphoning of calories directly from her body when she accessed her skills. By the time they had all finished lunch, she'd managed to consume a huge double cheeseburger and a bowl of chili.

Taylor left early to get started on the web search before Quinn got there. Miranda went with her, leaving Quinn with Naomi for the remainder of the meal. The vampire had ordered a mug of warm AB negative and sat sipping it while Quinn ate.

As she started on the chili, Quinn glanced at Naomi.

"You don't have to sit here with me. I'm fine to eat by myself."

"I have nowhere to be," Naomi replied.

"Suit yourself." Quinn went back to the tasty bowl of food.

"Quinn, I'm not disappointed in you, if you're worried about that."

She looked up. "Clark is, and you probably should be."

"Nonsense, Quinn. I've known Gemma for a long time. I got to know her when we were teenagers. She's always been the type of person who never made a move without figuring out every angle. If she came here and knew she had to challenge you, you can be sure she did her homework. She walked through those doors, already knowing what she needed to do to win. She used Avery in ways that magnified her strengths and your weaknesses."

"If you and Clark knew she would do things that way, why did you let her play the game and put me up against Avery in the first place?"

"Because we had to find out what she was up to. Clark and I have both been working behind the scenes to figure that out."

Quinn shook her head. "Not very successfully if I was the one to discover it."

Naomi nodded. "You're right. That's one of the reasons Clark is angry. I think he still hoped you'd win, even with Gemma cheating. Now he is playing from behind and at a disadvantage."

"You know," Quinn said. "I sometimes wish you two trusted me enough to fill me in on this stuff before everything goes to crap on us. Now I have to bust my ass to fix everything."

Naomi smiled. "Don't you prefer it that way? You always played better lacrosse when your team was behind at the half. You like a comeback win as much as anyone I've ever seen."

Quinn didn't like it when Naomi reminded her that she'd watched Quinn from a distance the whole time she grew up. It made her remember all the times she'd felt so alone in the world as a kid. That was a time when all she wanted was to have a real mother or father to take care of her.

She glared at the vampire. "This time, it's a whole lot more important than a stupid high school sporting event, Mother."

Quinn spotted a hint of a smile on Naomi's face at her response. Her anger flared until she realized why. This was the first time she'd used the word "mother" aloud when referring to her.

Shaking off her annoyance at herself, Quinn said, "Look, I can't shake the feeling something much bigger than a simple hidden artifact is in play here. Every time things get bad here in Baltimore, there's a Fae connection, and when we track it down, it points back to Princess Filippa. I talked to Aurora about it and—"

"I didn't know you went to her. Quinn, that's as dangerous as making a deal with Filippa. You're aware Aurora has her own agenda too, right?"

Quinn nodded. "I know. They all think we're just stupid, short-lived humans. Right now, she's got a reason to help me, so I took advantage of it. I figure as long as I have that dragon egg, Aurora will lend aid when it doesn't run counter to her own interests. Right now, she's all about messing with Filippa. I don't know what she has against the other princess, and I don't really care. I'll use it as much as I can until it changes."

"Fair enough," Naomi replied. "What did Aurora tell you?"

"That Filippa is focused on an alternate translation of the Huntress prophecy the former clan leaders relayed to me. This one reunites the Fae with their fallen cousins in the netherworld."

"My God!" Naomi exclaimed, shocked. "We just stopped Handon and his followers from what they were doing to allow demons a foothold here."

Quinn nodded. "And who was there watching the whole thing from the wings?"

"Filippa." Naomi bared her fangs as her anger slipped out from her usual iron-clad control.

"Uh-huh. And she seems willing to do just about anything she has to."

Naomi picked up her mug and drained it. She licked a bit of blood off her upper lip and stood up. "I'm going to go talk to Clark. He needs to know what you found out. You catch up with Taylor and see what you can discover about the Federal Hill area. I'll ask Clark, too. He might know some local lore we're not aware of that could help you figure out the location of this Crystal Well."

"Great. We can all meet up later and put our heads together."

Naomi nodded and left through the back door.

Quinn finished the last of her lunch in peace. She had a

lot swirling through her mind at the moment, and she knew somewhere in that jumble of thoughts was the one nugget of information that would bring all this together for her. Once she found it, she'd find a way to beat Gemma at her own game.

CHAPTER EIGHTEEN

Taylor had started the search and was well into the process by the time Quinn got there. She'd gone to her apartment and retrieved the old map she'd found in the bar that morning. It was possible Taylor would be able to use it to somehow find one of the hidden tunnel entrances, and that would lead Quinn to Gemma's operation here in Baltimore.

Taylor held the map up to the overhead light. "This thing is really old. The paper they used has too much acid in it, and it's about to crumble to bits."

"Can you use it?" Quinn asked. "It's the only clue I have, beyond what Aurora told me."

"We can try." Taylor got up and walked over to a table against the wall. Several devices and disassembled computer components lay on it.

She lifted the lid on one of the devices and laid the map on a plate of glass inside. Closing the lid, Taylor reached around back and grabbed a cable, uncoiling it and running it to the side of her main CPU on the floor by her work-station.

"What's that?" Quinn asked.

"A high-res scanner. There might be more detail there than we can pick up. It could be hidden by the age of the paper. The original ink has faded, and this might be able to bring it back." Taylor looked up from her computer at Quinn and smiled. "Fingers crossed."

She glanced back down, tapped a sequence of keys, and hit enter. The scanner started humming, and a sliver of bright white light escaped from beneath the lid as it went through the process of analyzing the map.

Taylor cracked her knuckles and said, "Okay, let's see what we've got here. She leaned forward and stared at the center monitor. Quinn moved around so she could see too, and Miranda hovered on the other side of the tech witch.

A few seconds later, a blown-up version of the map appeared on the screen. The quality of the scan magnified all the imperfections of the original map. At first glance, it didn't look like Taylor was going to discover anything new.

Taylor leaned closer and traced a finger across the screen. "Something used to be printed or written here." She turned to Quinn to make sure she was paying attention. "See, there's a faint outline beyond the base of the hill. I'm not sure what it represents, but let's see if I can use some different filters to help it stand out.

She used the touchpad to outline that area of the map and then clicked icons on the screen. Each one subtly changed the colors as if they were viewing through tinted lenses.

Taylor clicked through a bunch of options. She went so

fast, they almost missed the one that showed what they were looking for.

"Stop," Quinn said. "I saw something on that last one."

"I saw it. Hold on. Let me make an adjustment and go back."

The screen changed color again, and then the version of the map Quinn wanted appeared. "Look, by the faint line there. Are those words?"

"They look like it. Let's zoom in and see what they say. They're so small."

As the map grew larger and centered on the area of text. Quinn squinted at it. "It looks handwritten, not printed. Damn, I'm horrible at reading cursive script."

Miranda rolled her ghostly eyes and said, "I weep for the education system. What are they teaching you kids these days?"

"How to do useful things like using computers," Taylor replied. "We never would have seen this if it hadn't been for my awesome tech witch skills."

Miranda smiled. "It doesn't do any good if you can't read what's revealed."

"That's what spectral godmothers are for, right, T?" Quinn asked, grinning.

Miranda ignored the comment. "The note was written by whoever originally used the pamphlet. It reads, '*Old tunnel system for miners to access pits.*"

"What's that mean?" Taylor asked.

"'Pits' probably referred to the working parts of the mine where the silica was located," Miranda said. "Look, the line traces back to these areas in bolder print that denote the mine tunnels."

Quinn shrugged. "That doesn't help. I can't figure out how it fits today."

"Hold on," Taylor said. "Let me try something."

She tapped a few keys. On the left-hand screen, up popped a map of the city of Baltimore. Taylor zoomed in to look at the Federal Hill neighborhood. She looked back and forth between the two monitors as she fine-tuned the modern map's size.

At last, she nodded and, using her trackpad, dragged the modern map over the older map, adjusting it so it was semi-transparent. She rotated it to match the key landmarks.

Quinn pointed to the end of the faint line that showed the old tunnel access. "What's out here? I can't tell from the way you have the newer map."

"Here, try this," Taylor said. She dropped a flag at the location of the tunnel entrance on both maps and then dialed up the opacity of the modern map so Quinn could see it better as it was now. The flag stood out on a residential street south of the main part of Federal Hill.

"What's out there? Can you show me a street view?"

Taylor smiled. "Can I show you a street view? Do you doubt me, Quinn?"

"I was just asking. I don't know that part of the city too well. Something tickles my memory, but I can't put my finger on it."

Taylor opened up a browser window on her third screen and went back to the center screen to copy the address. In the browser window, she pasted the address in the search bar.

A few seconds later, an interactive map view showed all

the homes on the street as if seen from the sidewalk out front. Quinn asked, "Which one is the address we flagged?"

Taylor tapped an icon, and one of the homes was highlighted. The viewpoint moved until the house was centered on the screen.

"Of course," Quinn said. "I know that house. I can't believe it was this easy. I should have realized where it was leading me."

"What are you talking about?" Taylor asked.

Quinn stabbed a finger at a large Victorian home set back from the street behind a black wrought iron fence. "I know that home. It's the first place I met Filippa when I rescued her. It seems like forever ago, but I wouldn't forget it. I'm beginning to think she wasn't in any danger back then. It explains her flippant attitude toward our attempts to secure her safety when we thought the VirSync slayers were chasing her."

Miranda stared at the screen and said, "It *can't* be that easy."

"I know that's the right place," Taylor said, double-checking the address on the other screen. "If that old map is right, this is where the mine entrance is located. At least, it was before they were all sealed up. That's what you said happened to them, right, Quinn?"

"They were sealed," Quinn said. "By now, that tunnel entrance has been reopened by a group of kidnapped werebadgers. That's what all that action around Inez's restaurant was about. Gemma needed to ensure her miners stayed on task."

"It makes sense. Filippa was already working on this when we rescued her from the VirSync assassins."

"So, what next?" Taylor asked.

"I have to go there, T. There's no other option."

"If Gemma is running an operation there, she might be expecting you," Miranda said. "She's been one step ahead of us the whole time."

Quinn shook her head. "I don't think so. The look on her face back at the harbor when Avery beat me said she thought she'd won a final victory."

"If that's true," Taylor said, "you can't disappear now. You need to stick around and let her gloat about it. You have to appear beaten so she doesn't suspect what you plan on doing."

Miranda turned to Quinn. "Can you do that?"

"Do what?"

"Look beaten. I've never seen you look anything but defiant, even at the worst of times. Even when I died."

Quinn clenched her fists as the memory of the moment John Handon took Miranda's life right in front of her. She counted it among her greatest failures.

"Quinn," Miranda said. The ghost drifted around and floated in front of Quinn. "I didn't just say that to remind you of my death. Look at how you're carrying yourself right now."

Quinn glanced down. Her fists were clenched. Her whole body trembled, and she understood what Miranda was trying to get her to see. She inhaled and released a deep breath, forcing herself to relax.

Quinn smiled at Miranda. "I get the message. Don't worry. I can do this. I've got to keep my eyes on the prize, and that is getting to the heart of what Gemma is trying to do and stopping it. For that, I'll look like I've been defeated."

"You'd better," Taylor said. "We won't get a second chance. If Filippa has been using that house since we first went there, they have to be close to finding the way into the tunnels. They could be near the artifact already."

Quinn nodded. "I'm going to go take a shower and get ready. I'll see you both at dinner. We'll congratulate Avery on her success and welcome her as the new Huntress. Then I'm going to show them what a real Huntress does when there's trouble in her town."

CHAPTER NINETEEN

Avery wasn't in the apartment when Quinn went up. That was fine with her. She didn't feel like dealing with smug comments, or worse, condescension from the other girl.

Quinn jumped in the shower, taking her time. While she knew she had to go down and let Gemma and Avery take a victory lap over dinner, it didn't mean she looked forward to the experience. After she got dressed, she puttered around, using picking up dirty clothes and other clutter as an excuse not to go downstairs.

Her phone chirped with a message from Taylor.

We're at dinner. No sign of Gemma or Avery.

Quinn smirked. The two of them probably had a grand entrance planned for when the whole clan was present. They'd want to show off for the other members of the supernatural community in O'Malley's. Word would get around Baltimore about Avery's new status faster that way.

Taking a deep breath, Quinn slipped on her boots, made a last check in the mirror to make sure she looked good, and started downstairs. It was time to face the consequences of her failure, even if it was a way to hide what she had planned for later that evening. It wouldn't do to give Gemma and Avery a heads up that she was coming after them.

The two of them still hadn't arrived when Quinn got to the bar. The place was rocking. The band had the patrons up and dancing, even though it was early. The honky-tonk band played as Quinn walked to join her friends.

Clark, Naomi, Taylor, and Miranda sat at one of the larger round tables, waiting for her to arrive. Everyone already had their food. Quinn sat down next to Taylor and glanced at the two empty chairs across from her.

Juni came by to take her order, and after the waitress left, Quinn looked at the others. "Any sign of the guests of honor?"

Clark shook his head. "I tried calling Gemma. She's not answering."

Naomi said, "It's not like her to miss an opportunity to gloat. This is what she wanted, after all."

"What if it's not?" Quinn said.

"This is a huge win for Gemma," Clark stated. "Of course, it's what she wants."

Taylor raised her voice as the band started a new song. "Quinn's right. We did some checking around, and I think she's found something."

Quinn said, "Have you ever heard of something called the Crystal Well?"

Clark shook his head. "What does it have to do with Gemma and Avery?"

"It's some kind of arcane object of power, and I think

it's here in Baltimore. That's why Gemma and Avery came when they did. They're working for Filippa to find and obtain the Crystal Well for her."

Clark sighed. "Filippa isn't the boogeyman, Quinn. She's not behind everything that goes wrong in the world."

"Except, in this case, she is." Quinn stabbed a finger on the table in front of her. "She was the Fae sponsor who protected Avery after the purges. She financed Gemma so she could train the girl and maybe others to meet some alternate Huntress prophecy. She sent the two of them here to get in my way so she could keep looking for something she's been after since the very beginning."

"Quinn—" Clark began.

"Hear me out," Quinn said. "I've got proof. I managed to track down the likely location of the Crystal Well here in Baltimore. It's somewhere under Federal Hill. The entrance to the old tunnels and mines beneath that part of the city is located where we found Filippa the first time I met her."

Clark glanced at Naomi. "Okay, let's go back and start at the beginning. Tell us how you found all this out about Gemma and Avery."

Quinn went through everything she'd learned, both from her conversations with Avery and from Aurora. She let Taylor explain the things she'd found. Clark and Naomi asked questions to get clarification on a few details. Once she finished, Clark sat back and stared at her for a few seconds.

He frowned. "If this is true, it's not a good sign they didn't show up here for dinner. The only reason I can think of for them not to come is that they're close to finding what they came for."

"We need to be sure," Naomi urged.

"I can find out what they're doing tonight," Quinn said. "Let Taylor send me into the VR system. I'll scout the area around the house and get the proof we need to expose their plot."

Clark said, "Exposing them isn't enough. We have to make sure they don't find the talisman. We don't even know for sure what it does. We have to get to it first and take it before they do."

"All the more reason to let me go in," Quinn said. "I can slip into the tunnels and find out how close they are to locating it. Then I'll come back so we can plan our next move."

"Quinn," Naomi said, "your plan is good as long as you remember this is a scouting mission. If they have a werepanther pride providing muscle, you have to approach this with care. You can't go in there and think you'll be able to fight your way out again."

"I figured that out the hard way when I went to talk to Inez, remember?"

"Naomi's right," Clark warned. "Scouting for information only this time. Find out what you can and get out. Got it?"

Quinn nodded. "I can do this. You'll see. I'm more than just a badass fighting machine with a pretty face."

Clark didn't answer right away. It was several seconds before he gave a nod. Everyone pitched in with ideas at that point. If Quinn found what they expected her to, this would require all hands on deck. Eventually, the plan came together. Everyone got up and went to get started on the night's work. It was time to get some payback.

A half-hour later, Quinn sat on the table in Taylor's workroom, geared up and ready to go into the system.

Clark stood beside her. He placed a hand on her shoulder. "Scout only. No fighting. If they discover you, they'll know we're on to them."

"I've got this. I can do it."

Naomi said, "We don't doubt it, Quinn. We just don't want you to get distracted if you run into Avery. Now's not the time to prove you're better than her."

As much as Quinn itched for a rematch with the other Huntress, she knew they were right. "I told you I've got this. I'll come home, and we can all go back together, okay?"

Clark nodded. "Okay." He turned to the others. "Taylor, ready to send her in?"

"Ready to go. I've added a little something to the code to dial up your stealth abilities. It should show up on your scout menu as a drop-down selection."

"I'll let you know how it goes," Quinn said. She laid back and settled the VR headgear, lowering the goggles into place. "I'm ready."

Taylor tapped a few keys on her keyboard, then started chanting as she melded her spells with the computer code of the VR system.

The system tugged Quinn backward until she virtually fell through the table and into the blackness of the system's bridge between worlds.

CHAPTER TWENTY

Quinn arrived back in the park atop Federal Hill and dropped to one knee. She scanned the area from the shadows and saw no one out and about. It was late on a weeknight, so she wasn't surprised. She didn't want to rely on her stealth abilities until she absolutely had to engage them, not knowing how long she'd need to keep them going.

Rising to her feet, Quinn jogged to the edge of the park, where it bordered a residential neighborhood of brick row homes. Keeping to the shadows as much as possible, Quinn started working her way down the street on the left side, watching behind her for cars or pedestrians. It wouldn't do to be seen sneaking around or get caught in the headlights of a random passerby. People in this community would be quick to call the police on a suspected prowler.

Twice she had to stop and take cover for a car coming down the street. On one occasion, she ducked under a set of stone steps to hide as a gentleman in his fifties came out to walk his dog. Quinn held her breath so the dog wouldn't notice her and draw the man's attention to her presence. She waited several minutes after they passed to be sure they were gone.

She was glad she had. As Quinn was about to stand and return to the sidewalk, the man came back around the corner ahead of her, returning by the same route to his home. She barely made it back into hiding in time.

After they'd passed and she'd checked to make sure they'd gone inside, Quinn continued on her way. She was only a block or so away from the target house, according to her HUD map.

When she reached the end of the street, Quinn found a set of basement stairs recessed into the side of the home on the corner. From there, she could watch the Victorian home where she'd first met Filippa. Situated across the street this way, Quinn got a good look at the front of the home. There were a few lights on, but no other sign of people inside or out.

She couldn't just walk up to the front door and knock. It was unlikely she'd be able to sneak in the front door anyway. Both rooms at the front of the house on the first floor had their lights on. She'd be seen, or if her stealth abilities held up, someone would see the door open and close and know someone was nearby.

Quinn decided the best option was to try the back of the home and the kitchen entrance. Based on her memory of the last time she was there, the stairs to the basement started in the kitchen. She figured that was where she would find the tunnel entrance if there was one.

Before she headed out to work her way around the block to the rear, Quinn glanced at her HUD and brought up the ability icons. The arrow-shaped scout icon highlighted right away, blinking to show a new ability available. She'd forgotten that Taylor had added something to the system tonight.

Quinn concentrated on the flashing icon so the menu opened. The dropdown had her standard hide in shadows ability, which she'd already accessed with a command word. Below it was a new listing:

Enhanced Recon

Quinn concentrated on the listing without activating it to see if there was an explanation. She smiled when a pop-up appeared.

Enhanced Recon — Allows near invisibility along with limited scent and sound masking. Duration is sixty seconds. May be engaged two times per session.

That was perfect. Inez had been able to detect Quinn's presence by scent when she'd used her standard hide ability. This new skill would allow her to elude any shifters who might smell or hear her with their enhanced senses. She *was* worried about the time limitation. Sixty seconds wasn't very long. She'd have to plan carefully to avoid getting trapped in the open when it ran out.

Quinn tapped her earpiece. "T, I'm getting ready to go inside. I'm going to circle around and come in from the backyard."

"We're monitoring your position. Let us know if you need anything."

"Will do. Oh, and good work on the Enhanced Recon skill. I'll let you know how it works."

"Remember, it's time-limited."

"I saw that. I'll be careful. Okay, heading in. I'll be back in touch soon."

Quinn cut the connection and checked the street in both directions. A narrow side street opened up a few houses down from the target. The map indicated it connected to an alley that ran behind that part of the neighborhood.

She switched to satellite view and tried to dial in the magnification on the backyards along the alley. It looked like there were fences behind most of them. There was a shed or small detached garage in the yard behind the Victorian home. She might be able to get up on the roof of the shed and check out the home from the back before going in.

The coast was clear as she shifted her attention away from the HUD. Whispering, "mist," Quinn ran in a crouch across the street as the hazy outline touched the edge of her visual field. She stayed between the widely spaced street lamps to let the shadows do their thing. Anyone taking a casual glance at the street would see shifting shadows as if a breeze waved the leaves in the trees.

She'd angled her crossing to get her closer to the side street that led to the alley. Reaching the corner, Quinn put her back against the wall of the home and peeked around to check the other street.

It was a good thing she did. The smell of wet fur warned her of the approaching werepanthers before she saw them. Two tall men in leather biker jackets walked in her direction on the sidewalk.

Backing up along the front of the home, Quinn searched for somewhere to hide. She remembered how hard it had been to take down the werepanthers before and what Clark had told her about avoiding a fight.

Quinn's eyes fell on a grate in the sidewalk a few feet away. It had to lead to one of the storm drains to the harbor. It was the only option for a quick place to hide.

Spreading her fingers and shoving them into the grate's holes, Quinn tensed her muscles and dialed up her strength from the stamina bar. She tugged upward, and on the second pull, the grate came up. Tilting it to one side, Quinn slipped through the narrow opening and let the grate fall closed above her, catching it at the last instant to slow it so it dropped into place almost silently.

Just in time.

The two shifters rounded the corner and stared up and down the street.

The taller of the two said, "I heard something,"

"Me, too. Like metal scraping on metal?"

"Yeah. Just like that."

The two scanned the street while Quinn watched, peering up at the pair from only a few feet away. She should be able to hide down here until they went on their way. It was dark, and the musty smells of wet leaves and whatever else had washed through here during the last storm should cover her scent.

Up above, the two shifters searched the street for several minutes. After a final scan up and down, the shorter werepanther pulled out a big cigar and a silver lighter. He lit the stogie, flipped the lighter closed, and blew a series of smoke rings.

His partner walked over and held out a hand. The first

shifter reached into his pocket again and handed another cigar to his companion.

"Thanks. Are these the ones you got after shaking down that tobacco shop?"

"Yep. Nothing like a twenty-dollar cigar."

"Twenty dollars? Damn, that's a lot for a smoke."

"What do you care? As far as you and I are concerned, it's free. Lots more where this one came from. I arranged with the owner to slip me more of these when I came to collect, and he didn't have to come up with so much cash."

The taller one shook his head as he puffed on the second cigar. "Boss ain't gonna like it if he finds out you've been skimming on the protection racket."

"He's not gonna find out, right?"

"Not as long as few of these find their way to me from time to time."

The two of them chuckled and started walking up the street toward the Victorian home.

Quinn couldn't see them anymore, but she did pull them up on her HUD. They appeared as red dots on the overhead map. She wondered why they hadn't appeared on it originally and how many others hadn't shown up along with them. The good news was, now that she'd spotted them, they remained on the map, even though they'd moved out of sight.

She followed their progress as they walked away, trying to gauge the best time to slip out of the storm drain and make a run for the side street. She was about to make her move when a sound echoed from down the storm drain tunnel. It was faint, but it sounded like someone crying out in pain.

Quinn ducked and peered down the tunnel in both directions, but she couldn't see anything. It was almost pitch-black in here.

"Dammit, I need to see."

The instant she spoke the activation words, her inherent Huntress night vision switched on. The blackness of the tunnel was now gray-green, allowing her to see down the long rectangular passage. There was no one visible in the direction from which the noise came.

The tunnel was too small to stand up, so Quinn hunched over and started making her way down the tunnel, searching carefully as she went for the source of the voice. She headed more or less in the direction of her target. Could she be lucky enough for this to get her in somehow?

The answer was yes and no.

Quinn got to the point in the tunnel that was about even with the Victorian home above and stopped just short of a T-junction. The storm drain kept going parallel to the street above.

To the left, in the direction of the homes on that side, a large, round concrete pipe joined the even larger storm drain. Quinn stared up the pipe, straining her ears as she stood at the opening, trying to quiet her breathing and beating heart so she could hear if anyone was down there.

The pipe angled down, so she could only see about twenty feet before it turned out of sight to the left. Whimpering drifted up to her, much clearer this time. She was definitely closer. The voice sounded like muffled groaning. It was louder than before, but still faint.

"Man, I don't like this," Quinn said, trying to judge the

diameter of the opening. She couldn't tell if her mind was playing tricks on her. It looked to her like the circular pipe narrowed farther down.

Another whimpering groan made up her mind. Quinn bent over and climbed into the opening. There was enough room for her to crawl at this point, although her back scraped the top. Quinn ignored the muck squishing between her fingers and soaking the knees of her jeans as she moved forward.

Her eyes hadn't fooled her. The pipe did narrow as she continued. Luckily it wasn't enough to force her down so far that she had to crawl on her belly. It did make her assume a sort of moving plank position on elbows and knees.

Quinn reached the point where the pipe angled down and to the left. When she stopped and listened, faint breathy gasps came from up ahead. Peering forward, Quinn could make out a dark shape in the tunnel, filling half the pipe. It looked more like a pile of rags than a person.

Reaching to her side, Quinn drew her Bowie knife while she had the room to do so and resumed her advance. The moaning form was only about fifteen feet away.

Taking a chance, Quinn whispered, "Hey, I heard you cry out. Are you okay?"

The rag pile moved and then rolled over. A furry face appeared, with a white stripe from the forehead back and down the neck amidst the brownish hair.

"Who are you?" the creature hissed. It bared its fangs and tried to look fierce. The pale face and slack skin told Quinn the shifter was injured.

"Easy does it. I'm a friend." Quinn recognized it as a werebadger, maybe one of the missing ones they'd been looking for. That confirmed their suspicions about this location if the presence of the bikers above didn't already do that.

"If you're a friend, why are you pulling a knife on me?"

Quinn lowered her Bowie but didn't sheathe it. "Hey, you never know who you're going to meet in these tunnels, am I right?"

When the creature didn't respond, Quinn said, "Look, I know Inez Huckle. I came looking for her after some goons kidnapped her."

"You know Inez? I heard them threatening to bring her in before I tried to escape. I knew it couldn't be a good thing if they'd decided to be so bold and take our clan leader."

"You were right. That's why I came. I'm Quinn. The Huntress? Have you heard of me?"

"You're the one who took out that vampire coven a few months back. Funny, you don't look that tough."

"Hey, I'm here, aren't I? I don't think you have a lot of choice about who rescues you."

The werebadger shifted and groaned as it rolled over. Quinn still couldn't tell if it was a male or a female here in the tight confines of the pipe.

"You're hurt. How bad is it?"

"Bad enough that I decided I was going to die here in this sewer pipe."

Quinn made a snap decision and sheathed her blade, then shifted forward a few feet. "Show me where you're hurt. Maybe I can help."

"Now you're a healer, too?" The werebadger's tone dripped suspicion.

Quinn didn't take offense. Instead, she smiled and said, "Maybe. You have any other options?"

The werebadger grinned, showing a mouthful of sharp teeth. "You make a good point, Huntress."

When it rolled all the way over onto its back, Quinn could see it was a female and at least ten years older than her. The move revealed a chest and belly covered in blackened and putrid claw wounds. The stench was overpowering now that the wounds were uncovered.

"How long have you been injured?"

"I've been holed up in this pipe for two days now. The werepanther I jumped messed me up pretty good. He won't be bothering anyone else, though. I ripped out his throat while he was clawing me."

Quinn remembered learning about the savage determination of badgers in the animal world. It seemed their shifter kin were no different.

She slid closer and tried not to wrinkle her nose at the smell. She didn't want to offend the dying woman. "What's your name?"

"Gretchen."

"Well, Gretchen, I've got an idea, but I have to warn you, I've never done this before. It's something I've only seen done. I've been told I have the ability, though."

"It's not like I have a lot of options at this point. I had resigned myself to die in here and be discovered as a bare skeleton by city works crews years from now."

"Well, let's see if we can avoid that. This might hurt a little."

"It can't hurt more than it does now. Do your worst."

Quinn nodded and stretched out her hands, hovering them over the woman's chest and belly. She tried to remember what Avery had done when she'd healed Quinn's shoulder after the werepanther fight.

She reached out with her mind to search the area for ley lines close enough to draw upon. It was an instinctive reaction when she wanted to power up. Then Quinn remembered Avery had said the power to heal came from within the Huntress, not without.

Redirecting her mind inward, Quinn pulled up her HUD and drew down her stamina bar as she tried to put that energy, not into her strength or reaction speed like she usually did, but into a flow of healing energy.

At first, nothing happened. For several seconds, Quinn squeezed her eyes shut and trembled all over as she tried to force her energy into Gretchen's injured body.

A voice, as familiar as it was distant, flowed into her mind. It was the voice of the woman clan leader or goddess or whoever spoke to her at certain times. Quinn stopped straining to force her energy outward so she could try to make out what the distant voice said.

"Nature is health, nature is flow, not force. Let the power flow from you, Huntress."

Quinn stopped and relaxed, and Gretchen looked at her. "I don't think it worked. Don't worry about it. You tried."

"No," Quinn said. "I think I was doing it wrong. Don't give up while I try again."

Quinn closed her eyes again, but this time she tried to focus on the energy in her stamina bar as a flowing river, using that imagery instead of something solid she had to force or push out. This time, she imagined a channel through which the energy would flow down her arms and into her hands. She didn't force or direct the power to do anything. She just let it do what nature wanted it to.

It worked.

Gretchen and Quinn drew sharp breaths at the same time. A flaring, searing heat flashed from Quinn's hands, and the whole tunnel lit up for an instant with the power of the flow.

When it died down and Quinn drew her hands back, she could tell Gretchen's breathing had eased. It no longer had the raspy quality indicating fluid in the lungs and throat.

The werebadger let out a long sigh. "Oh, my, that is much better."

Quinn studied the area where the wounds were located. She couldn't tell if they were better or not. The crusted blood and torn fabric of the woman's clothes still clung, but the putrid stench seemed to have dissipated.

"How do you feel?" Quinn asked.

"It still hurts a little, but the throbbing ache is gone from my gut, and I can move without pain now."

As if to test her statement, she rolled back to her stomach and lifted herself up onto her hands and knees. "See, I could barely crawl far enough to get in here earlier."

"Good, I'm glad." Quinn smiled. She realized the healing spell or whatever it was had filled her with a sense of fulfillment and peace. Maybe it was an aftereffect of doing what she had done. Her stamina bar had already started to refill with energy. That was much faster than it had when she'd pulled power from it before.

Gretchen pointed up the pipe toward where the storm drains ran along the street. "If you back up, we can get out of here, now that I am mobile again."

Quinn shook her head. "You came from the tunnels below here, didn't you?"

The werebadger nodded.

"Then I can't leave. I have to go down there." She pointed past Gretchen.

The older woman shook her head. "There's all kinds of trouble that way, kid. You should get out and come back with help."

"I'll be okay, I'm just here to scout things. I have to try to see what's going on. Anything you can tell me about what's happening down there would be helpful, too."

Gretchen glanced back down the pipe and shook her head. "It's your funeral. Look, I don't know much. They're looking for something, but none of us knows what it is. Some big dark-haired lady came down there a couple of times in the last week or so. She pulled out a folded map. I never got a good look at it, but she used it to tell the panthers where she wanted us to dig next."

"I think I know what they're after. Are you sure they haven't found it yet?"

Gretchen shook her head. "Not as of two days ago, at least. The lady was yelling the last time she was in there. I got the impression she was in a hurry because the werepanthers put a beating on us and made us work extra hard. That was when I decided to try to get out."

Quinn smiled. "Well, now you're out. If I lie flat against

one side of the pipe, do you think you can wriggle past me?"

"Oh, easily. You sure you won't come along?"

"No," Quinn said. "I need to see this for myself. I'll be out as soon as I scout around a little. In the meantime, do you know where O'Malley's pub is on the east side of the city?"

"I've heard of it."

"Can you go there and ask for Clark or Naomi? They'll be able to get you more help with your injuries, and you can tell them how to get into this tunnel system. That way, if I do get stuck or caught, they'll know how to come find me."

"Fair enough." Gretchen crawled forward as Quinn pressed herself against the side of the pipe.

As soon as the werebadger was past her, Quinn called, "Be careful. There were a pair of werepanthers patrolling up there. Try to make your way farther out in the storm drains before you exit the tunnels."

"Thanks," Gretchen replied. "You be careful, too."

Quinn nodded and turned back to look down the now-empty pipe. Gretchen had described how she'd found the entrance to the pipe where it opened into a cave off the main tunnel. Quinn would have to wriggle back through the same route until she reached the fresh excavations by Gemma's kidnapped werebadgers.

With a deep breath to steel her determination, Quinn started crawling, angling downward, deeper into the tunnels beneath the city.

CHAPTER TWENTY-ONE

"What do you mean, you've lost the tracking data stream?"

Taylor leaned forward, furiously tapping on her keyboard. Worry wrinkled her brow. "Just hold on, Clark. I'll tell you as soon as I figure it out. Yelling isn't going to make it happen faster."

She hit enter and watched the screen to see if it reconnected to Quinn's stream. The comm had lost the connection soon after she'd called in to tell them her plan.

A few minutes later, the normal brainwave stream flowing through the VR system had stopped. There'd been no sign of distress; it had just cut off. It could be caused by a lot of things, but the consequence was the same. She couldn't recall Quinn until she re-established the link.

Under normal circumstances, Taylor could see when stress levels reached a critical point. She could see when Quinn was in a fight. That hadn't happened this time. If it had, she could've run a crash recall and pulled Quinn out.

Under normal circumstances.

Somehow, they'd lost the signal. That had never happened before, but Taylor was certain she could find a workaround to reconnect to her friend. She just needed to relax and solve the problem using logic and maybe a touch of magic.

Of course, having Clark breathing down her neck made it hard to stay focused. When he put a hand on the back of her chair and leaned over to watch what she was doing, Taylor had enough.

"Do you want to sit down here and do it yourself? If you think you can do better, be my guest." Taylor swiveled the seat in Clark's direction and stood up.

Clark's face reddened, and he took in a deep breath in preparation for his reply to the tech witch.

Naomi stepped between the two of them. "Both of you, stop it. My daughter's in trouble, and the two of you starting a pissing match over who's going to save her isn't going to solve anything."

She turned to Taylor, who stood with her arms crossed, glaring at Clark. "Sit down, Taylor. Get back to work. You're our best chance of getting her back in one piece."

Taylor shifted her gaze to Naomi. The vampire's eyes glowed red, irises blazing with an inner light. Taylor nodded, then inhaled slowly and blew out the breath, working to calm herself.

Taylor sat down and swung the chair back around. She leaned over the keyboard and scanned the monitors to make sure the data hadn't shifted in the time her eyes had been off them.

Even with her attention on the computer, Taylor didn't miss catching a glimpse of Clark's fists held rigid at his sides. His knuckles had turned white from the pressure.

Naomi noticed, as well. "Clark, center yourself and get back in control. Think about what we can do next."

Miranda hovered nearby and said, "She's right. Quinn's been in tough spots before, and she's always found a way through. This is probably just a technical glitch."

"We can't be sure," Clark said. "Until we know one way or the other, we have to plan for the possibility that she's in trouble."

Naomi nodded. "You're right. We need to head down there."

"I was thinking of going by myself," Clark countered. "I work better alone."

"Not a chance. This is a clan, and it will be a team effort. That's what Quinn is building here. She would want us to work together."

When Clark didn't immediately say no, Naomi continued, "It's nighttime, so it's also the perfect time for me to go out with you."

"It'll be light in eight hours," Clark said. "What if we're still waiting in the car for an opening to go in after her?"

"You've got a trunk, don't you?"

Clark smiled. "You'll let me stuff you in the trunk of my car while it's daylight?"

"No," Naomi said. "But I'll climb in on my own so we can stay on location until the right time to enter."

Taylor clicked the menu and selected the option to restart the VR system in an attempt to reconnect with Quinn on boot-up. As the screen went dark and the boot sequence started, she turned to face the others.

"I think it's a great idea for you both to head down there. She might just have gone far enough underground to block the signal. From what I can see, the signal got progressively weaker until it cut off. I'm running a diagnostic to be sure. I'll have a better idea once it reboots."

Taylor slid in her chair to the side and pulled open the bottom drawer of a small filing cabinet beside her. If her suspicion was right, they might be able to boost their signal by putting a repeater transmitter on site. The VirSync engineers must have thought they'd need it someday because she had found a prototype repeater in the gear they'd recovered.

Taylor dug through the bundles of wire and circuit boards for the device. "Ah, got it!"

She pulled out a stacked pair of circuit boards wrapped in a length of shielded copper wire.

"Got what?" Naomi asked.

"I have a way we might be able to reconnect with her, but I need the two of you to get this signal booster as close to the tunnel entrance as you can. We might be able to use it to reconnect the system to her and maybe even relink our comms."

"What are the chances it'll work?" Clark asked, taking the proffered device and turning it over in his hand to study it. "Where's it plug in?"

"No plug," Taylor said. "But you'll need a battery pack. She rummaged through the drawer until she pulled out a pair of D-cell batteries held together by a tight wrapping of electrical tape.

Taylor held out her hand for the repeater. Clark returned it to her, and she slid the batteries into place so they were wedged between the two circuit boards. Then she connected two loose wires to the terminals on one of the circuits. The red LED on the top board switched on, and Taylor glanced at the right-hand screen to make sure the signal registered.

With a nod of confirmation, she handed it back to Clark. "Take that to Federal Hill. I'll tell you if you're close enough to connect to her."

Clark shoved the repeater into the side pocket of his long black duster, then pulled his car keys out of another pocket and turned to Naomi. "You coming?"

"Try to stop me."

Naomi didn't wait for Clark's reply. She moved to the door and went out into the hallway beyond.

Clark nodded and started after her. Over his shoulder, he called, "Keep in touch with us. We'll let you know what we see when we get there."

Taylor didn't say anything. She'd already turned back to her screens and began working on tuning the VR system and the magic that melded with it so she could try to catch up with her friend. After all, she was the clan's tech witch, and it was up to her to make this right.

CHAPTER TWENTY-TWO

"Dammit." For the second time, Quinn had cracked her head on a low-hanging rock jutting from the roof of the rough stone tunnel.

She scanned the way forward in the dim gray-green light her night-vision afforded in near-total darkness. Without it, she wouldn't have been able to navigate this narrow tunnel. It was a wonder Gretchen had made it as far as she did into the concrete pipe above.

Laying her head on her dusty forearm, Quinn paused for a few seconds. She had to press onward at this point. There was no way to turn around in the confined space, so her only option was to keep going down.

As she rested, a distant voice reached her. It was so faint, there was no way she'd have heard it if she'd been moving. Quinn couldn't make out what they said, but it came from the direction in which she headed.

Gaining a boost in energy from the excitement that she might be close to getting out of the tight confines of this cave, Quinn picked up her pace as much as she could. She couldn't push too fast without risking getting stuck.

The voice ahead turned into multiple voices. They grew louder as she moved downward in the sloped tunnel. Occasional cries of pain now reached her, interspersed with shouting and animal-like roars. Based on that combination, she expected werepanthers and the werebadger miners, too.

Quinn slowed her descent as soon as she realized a faint light filtered into the gap ahead of her. She had to be almost to the outlet of this tunnel.

Wriggling through one of the narrowest gaps yet, Quinn finally reached an area that opened up enough for her to sit upright and take stock of herself.

Quite a few scrapes and bruises adorned her skin where it was visible. A few thick locks of brown hair had fallen free of her ponytail. Reaching back, Quinn pulled the elastic free, letting her hair fall to her shoulders. She gathered it up again and used the band to re-secure it. If she had to fight, she didn't want her hair getting in the way.

Quinn shook her head at the last thought. "No fighting, Quinn. Remember?" she muttered to herself. There would be no way to get help if she got caught in a running battle down here. The best option was to stick to her scouting mission.

Finishing her brief rest, Quinn leaned forward, happy to have enough room to crawl on her hands and knees for a change. The light ahead grew brighter as she continued, illuminating more of the tunnel.

She turned a corner and stopped, finding herself inside a jagged crack that opened into a rectangular stone tunnel.

Quinn heard voices to the left but saw no one. They sounded pretty far off.

Quinn leaned out into the tunnel and looked both ways. There were electric lights attached to the wooden supports that had been placed in the tunnel to keep it from caving in. A long black wire connected the lights leading up the sloped tunnel to the right.

Opening her HUD, Quinn tried to see if her map function was working. Once she'd moved underground, it would only show her where she'd been and not the layout of the tunnels around her.

As the transparent overlay dropped into place, Quinn saw only the tunnels leading to the storm drain. She'd be able to find her way back to where she'd been and could climb back out that way if she had to. Nothing was shown, other than what she could see from her current vantage point. She tried to get her bearings in relation to the surface layout.

If her reckoning was correct, the way to the right led back toward the area beneath the Victorian home. The left-hand branch moved in the direction of the tallest part of Federal Hill. The latter was the direction from which she'd heard the voices.

Quinn climbed down from the gap in the tunnel wall and listened carefully. The voices had quieted for the time being. They could have moved down the tunnel or perhaps resumed their work of clearing the way.

She was here to scout the area, and Quinn decided to move to the left. There she could get an idea of how close the miners were to Gemma's objective. She dipped into the shadows again by whispering "mist" as she moved with caution deeper into the tunnel system.

Quinn kept her right hand on the tunnel wall, staying close to that side. She stopped in the shadows between the lights and listened as she went along the curving passage. She didn't want to surprise anyone.

In her HUD, Quinn double-checked that the scout icon was still illuminated so she could access the new Enhanced Recon skill. She felt like an opportunity to use it might come up soon.

As she dismissed the HUD, Quinn's nose caught a hint of wet fur. Soon after, the voices picked up again. Judging by the gruff shouts and whimpers, there were werepanthers ahead, driving the miners to dig.

Quinn hugged the inside wall of the curving tunnel. She half-expected to be surprised by someone coming along the tunnel at any moment.

She wasn't wrong.

Only because her basic stealth mode was engaged and she stood between two widely spaced lights did she avoid detection as a pair of werepanthers strode up the tunnel. The two had changed into humanoid panther form, although they still wore their leather biker jackets over their t-shirts and jeans.

Quinn crouched in the deepest of the shadows and held very still. She gripped the hilt of her Bowie in case it came to a fight. The pair talked as they passed.

"The boss ain't happy with our progress, and now the little buggers won't dig any farther because someone saw a ghost or something. I don't know why you didn't keep trying to drive them onward. You should've made an example of one to make the others keep going."

The second shifter said, "I'd already beaten one of them bloody and damn near unconscious. If that wasn't going to make them dig, I don't see how nearly killing all of them is going to help us. There aren't any of them left to add to the crew as it is. We've lost too many to the cave-ins."

"All I know is, you're calling her this time, not me."

"I want to try something first," the first one said. "We caught that clan mother or whatever she is. Let's bring her down and threaten her. Maybe that'll get them digging again, if only to save her life."

"It's your funeral. You know we have to keep her alive for some rite the boss has planned."

"Yeah, but they don't know that. Here's what we'll do…"

Quinn tried to hear the rest of the plan as they kept going up the passage. She was tempted to follow so she could listen in. They had to be talking about Inez. If she could free the werebadger matriarch, maybe it would cause an uprising or something with the miners.

On second thought, though, Quinn changed her mind. She wanted to get a look at the work crew and see what was going on where they were digging.

Resuming her careful approach, Quinn reached a point where she could see an open intersection ahead. The four-way crossing had only been partially excavated. The left- and right-hand tunnels were filled with rubble that had been hauled out of the area directly ahead.

It looked like a narrow gap had been opened to an area just beyond the intersection. Quinn couldn't see what was through there, but that was where all the attention was focused.

Five werepanthers, all partially shifted into cat form, stood over a huddled group of dirty miners. She looked around for some evidence of picks or shovels but didn't see any. Then she realized the shifted werebadgers were using the powerful claws at the ends of their sturdy little arms.

The leading werepanther stood peering into a cracked opening. "I don't see no ghosts or nothing else. What I do see is an opening into an older passage. That sounds like what we're looking for."

One of the cowering werebadgers pointed at the gap and said, "I saw it. It looked like an old miner wearing a hat with an old oil lamp clipped to it. He warned me the passage wasn't safe and then disappeared. I can't go in there, not if it's inhabited by the dead. We've had so many cave-ins already. We can't lose anyone else."

"Sure, you can," the looming werepanther said. "Because if you don't, my pals are gonna come back and start killing you, just like your little friend there."

He gestured at a crumpled body on the ground by the freshly dug opening. Anger welled up in Quinn and she fought to push it back down. She wanted to run down there and start showing those big cats what a real adversary could do to them.

Quinn took a deep breath and calmed herself. She had to figure out her next move. There was something through that gap, and the werepanthers seemed to think it was what Gemma had been looking for. She couldn't let that happen.

Studying the gap, Quinn figured she could make her

way through the narrow opening if she had a few seconds to contort herself the right way. It looked like they'd already started shoring up the area around it with wooden planks so the miners could widen the opening.

Judging the distance from her position to the opening, Quinn figured she could make it past the huddled miners and the guards with enough time left to get through the opening before sixty seconds were up. That meant she could use her Enhanced Recon ability to get in and check out the far side, then use it again on the way back out so she could get back to the surface.

Quinn edged as close to the brightly lit area as she dared, then opened her HUD and clicked on the scout arrow icon. From the open menu, she selected **Enhanced Recon** and closed it.

Immediately a countdown timer began running. That surprised her. She'd thought she would be able to start it sometime after she selected it. She lost valuable seconds before realizing the time had started.

Moving from her place in the shadows, Quinn walked at a smooth pace into the middle of the intersection. No one paid any attention to her, and she smiled. This was going to be easy.

Quinn wove between the guards and around the scattered miners seated on the ground until she stood next to the opening. A glance at the HUD told her she had ten seconds left.

Lifting her leg, she slid it through the lowest part of the gap in the tunnel wall until it reached the other side. She reached up and gripped one of the shoring timbers and pulled on it to haul herself through the opening. As she did, the wooden support beam shifted, and a few large rocks slid past her into the intersection.

"Hey, that board moved," one of the werepanthers said.

"It's the ghost," a bunch of the miners shouted as they crab-walked away from the gap.

Quinn bit back a curse and pulled harder to shift her body, now wedged in the narrow crack. Time ran down, and she still hadn't gotten through.

Two of the werepanthers moved toward the opening, peering into the gap in which Quinn was stuck. They had almost reached her.

Pulling at the wooden supports on both sides for leverage, Quinn heaved herself free and shoved herself the rest of the way through the opening as her timer hit zero. The force of her push was too much for the hastily placed supports, and the timbers on both sides came loose.

Quinn rolled over. Two werepanthers stared in at her, their eyes wide. They clearly saw her on the other side. Before they could act on what they saw, rocks dropped from the ceiling. Both shifters had to jump back from the gap as a substantial collection of rocks and dirt cascaded from the ceiling. The sudden cave-in drove them the rest of the way out of the opening. The rocks and dirt poured down on Quinn, too.

She rolled to her stomach and scrambled with hands and feet to move from where she lay. It was too late. The initial cascade of dirt and rocks pinned her legs to the ground. The rest of the avalanche rolled over her as she covered her head with her arms. With the cascade of dirt came darkness.

CHAPTER TWENTY-THREE

Quinn woke and gasped, inhaling a cloud of dirt. She coughed for almost a minute as she struggled to clear her throat. She tried to move and found she could lift her head a little, clearing some of the dirt from around her face. She attempted to lift herself up, but something pinned her to the ground from the shoulders down.

Clearing her throat, Quinn croaked out through the dust caking her mouth, "Dammit, I need to see."

The gray-green haze lit the darkness around her, and she got her first good look at the area she'd entered through the gap in the wall. Worked stone sheathed the curved walls, which formed an oval about twenty feet across at the widest point. Another tunnel led away from this room at the far end of the oval, opposite her position.

Twisting her neck so she could see behind her, Quinn spotted what held her down. Dirt and stone from the cave-in covered her to a depth of several feet, starting at her shoulders and extending to where the gap used to be.

Quinn pulled her arms around even with her shoulders and tried to push upward and lift her upper body from the pile trapping her. Some of it shifted away, letting her lift up down to her waist.

She spent long minutes pushing dirt and stones away to try to clear the pile from around her torso. After clearing everything she could reach while on her stomach, Quinn tried to roll onto her back.

Her legs wouldn't budge, though. Quinn tapped her earpiece, attempting to connect with Taylor back at O'Malley's. She heard a crackle on the comm but not the familiar chime of it connecting. "Taylor, can you hear me? I'm trapped in a cave in beneath Federal Hill. Are you there, T?"

She waited for a reply but got nothing back. She must be too far underground for the comm system to reach. It looked like she was on her own. She cleared more of the dirt from around her waist until she was too tired to keep going.

Sighing and lying back down, Quinn crossed her arms under her forehead. She ran through her options, saying aloud, "This is a mess."

"It sure is. I'm surprised you were able to dig out as much as you were."

Quinn lifted her head, scanning the room with her night vision to locate the source of the voice. She saw no one.

"Who's there?" Quinn said. "Show yourself."

She feared one of the werepanthers had somehow gotten through to her side before the cave-in sealed the opening. What revealed itself wasn't what she expected, though.

A form shimmered into view. Standing midway between her and the opening at the far end of the room was a man about four and a half feet tall. A faint blue nimbus of light surrounded his transparent form. He wore woolen pants, a collarless button-down shirt, and a vest. A leather hat was perched atop his head, with some sort of lamp attached to it. A yellow flame glowed inside.

"You're the ghost," Quinn said. "The one the miners talked about outside."

The man chuckled and smiled. "I suppose I am. At least, I'm one of them." He pointed at Quinn. "That was exactly what happened to me down here. I guess if we wait long enough, you'll be joining me."

Quinn grunted and shook her head. "Nope. No way am I dying down here, trapped in the dark like some kind of animal."

"It's not so bad as an afterlife goes. No one bothers you. Well, not usually."

"I don't care," Quinn insisted. She twisted again and started pulling at the dirt and rocks piled around her waist. "I'm getting out of here. I'm not becoming some moldy old ghost."

"Hey, I'm not moldy!"

"Sorry. No offense intended."

The man shrugged. "It's all right. Some of my friends are a little moldy, but you didn't hear me say it."

Despite her situation, Quinn smiled. "I'm Quinn. What's your name?"

"Upwood. Upwood Shires, at your service." He gave a little bow and finished with a flourish of one hand.

"Nice to meet you, Upwood. You sure have those miners out there pretty worked up. What did you do to scare them like that?"

"I can look like this, or I can look like a half-decayed corpse. I showed them the corpse-y version to try to keep them from coming in here."

"Why try to keep them away? Are you a guardian?"

"Oh, no. Why would you say something like that?"

Whatever she'd done to upset him, Upwood had become more than a little flustered.

He stammered as he continued, "Uh, um, I was just trying to warn them that the ceiling in this area is extremely unstable. It killed a whole bunch of my friends and me. Any digging is likely to set it off. That was why they gave up mining here."

Quinn glanced at the cave-in. "Do you think they'll be able to dig their way in here soon?" She didn't want to be trapped like this when the werepanthers came through the gap.

Upwood laughed. "It'll take them a few days at least to get in that way. The bulk of the cave-in went the other way. You're lucky it did, missy, or you'd be glowing like me right now."

Quinn took comfort from that and went back to digging to try to free her legs. She couldn't do anything else until she was free.

It turned out Upwood was good company. It took Quinn almost two hours to dig herself out. By the time she finally managed to drag herself clear, her legs had been trapped for a long time. She rubbed them, gasping in pain from the pins and needles sensation as the circulation returned to her lower extremities.

Upwood stood beside her, watching as she sat there rubbing her legs. "You sure do have gumption. I was sure you'd give up and let yourself be trapped down here with me."

"I'm not the type to give up, not ever."

Upwood cackled and waggled his finger at her. "I can see that. I can see that very well indeed." He hooked his thumbs in the pockets on the front of his vest. "So, missy, what's next? You gonna wait for your friends to dig you out?"

"They're not my friends. Well, the ones in charge aren't." She sniffed the air. "Strange that I can still smell them, even after the cave-in."

Upwood took a step back and said, "I'm glad you aren't with them. I don't like folks who hang around with werepanthers. They don't seem to have changed much since my day, though they didn't come into the city often."

Quinn cocked her head to one side and studied Upwood again. "You're a werebadger, aren't you? Maybe I'm catching a whiff of you? I didn't know ghosts carried smells."

The little man smiled and shifted into his badger form and back again. "You're a smart one, I'll give you that. I'd guess being a ghost is about smell as well as sight for someone of your obvious abilities. Tell me something—if you're not friends with those panthers, what are you doing down here?"

"I'm a Huntress. I came to see what they're digging for

and to try to stop them so the miners, your kin, could be set free."

"Oh, ho, a Huntress, you say? I can't say as I've ever seen one of your kind before. I knew a few men and women from the Hunter clan hereabouts. They were a scary sort, but they generally left a man to his own devices as long as he didn't harm normal human folk."

"The Hunters are mostly gone nowadays," Quinn said. "I'm trying to bring them back, and better than they were before."

"Given what I've seen you do in the short time since I met you, I wouldn't bet against you."

Quinn liked this little ghost miner. If she was going to be trapped down here in the dark for a while, there were worse people she could've been stuck with.

Quinn rubbed her legs until the ache disappeared and then stood and studied the room. "Upwood, what's down that way?" She pointed at the far end of the chamber.

"It's a passage to a special place, but it's protected, Quinn. You don't want to go down there. It's dangerous."

"Why, what's protecting it?"

"Oh, I have no idea," Upwood said. "I can't leave this area. I guess it's because this is where the cave-in killed me."

"So, you just hang around here by yourself? That must be horrible."

The little ghost shrugged. "It's not so bad. I tell myself stories, and when there's no one here, I think I kind of hibernate like bears in the wintertime."

"When was the last time you had anyone down here to talk to or haunt or whatever it is you do?"

"Oh, let's see. It would have to be just after the war between the states. There was a glassworks nearby that mined here for silica. If there was any light in here to reflect, you'd see the stone lining the walls sparkles. It's just about the prettiest sight in the world."

"Wow, that was over a hundred fifty years ago," Quinn said. She looked at the only exit from the chamber. "So, how do you know there's something dangerous down there if you've been stuck in here all this time?"

"Because a few years later, a guy who went down there came running back out bloody and screaming. He didn't stop to tell me what it was that did that to him, but he was pretty big and strong, so I figure it must be even bigger and stronger."

"When was this?" Quinn hooked a finger over her shoulder at the cave in. "When those guys opened the tunnel again?"

"Oh, no, way before that. This guy and some friends came in here. They couldn't see me like you can. They talked all about how they'd survived the 'Great War,' and now they were going to get rich because they'd found a map leading here."

"You said one guy ran out screaming. What happened to the others in his group?"

Upwood shrugged. "I guess whatever chewed up the big guy got the others. Lots of screaming and then nothing. Like I said, dangerous. Much too dangerous for a little thing like you, missy."

"Hey, I'm taller than you. Besides, I'm pretty dangerous when I want to be."

Upwood shook his head. "Suit yourself. Do me a favor before you go in there and die?"

Quinn bit back a snarky answer, feeling sorry for the lonely ghost. "Tell me a little bit about the world outside. I haven't seen a sunrise or sunset in so long."

She smiled, glad she'd held her tongue. "Sure, although I think things are a lot different than you're used to. We don't use horses and carriages to get around anymore. We have cars. They're a sort of wagon driven by engines. They go much faster, too. Oh, and we can fly now, as well."

Upwood chuckled. "Now you're just pulling an old miner's leg. How do you fly? I don't see no wings growing out of your back."

"I don't mean people fly. We have machines like the cars, but they have wings and carry people all over the world in just a few hours."

Upwood stared at her for a long time and then smiled. "I can't tell if you're kidding."

"Cross my heart," Quinn said, drawing a big X on her chest with one finger. "Hope to die if I'm lying."

"Dying's what ye'll be doing once you go down that tunnel."

"That was over a hundred years ago, too. The 'Great War' you said they mentioned? I think it was what we call 'World War One.'"

"There was more than one?" Upwood asked.

Quinn nodded. "Two, and a Cold War that wasn't a war at all, just a sort of staring contest." She pointed at the opening. "That happened so long ago that anything that killed those men must be long dead."

"You might be right. I can see I'm not going to convince

ya otherwise. I'll remember your name to tell it to the next fool who comes through here."

"You do that, Upwood. Who knows? Maybe if I die in there, I can come back as a ghost and keep you company for a while."

The old ghost smiled. "That would be mighty nice."

Quinn reached into her jacket and pulled out her Bowie, then waved at Upwood and stepped toward the chamber's remaining exit.

CHAPTER TWENTY-FOUR

Quinn swallowed hard as she left Upwood behind. Her mind wound through a variety of potential creatures that could be waiting ahead, each worse than the last. At last she stopped and took a deep breath, examining the passage around her.

The old mine tunnel had been lined with worked blocks of stone on the walls and ceiling. Thick wooden timbers supported the walls and roof every ten to fifteen feet.

With no sign to indicate what sort of guardian waited for her, she glanced back the way she'd come. There were no bones of the vanquished or dried bloodstains on the floor, nothing to indicate anything dangerous. Quinn wondered if Upwood had been telling her the truth.

It didn't matter. Quinn couldn't go back the way she came, and she also couldn't wait for the miners on the other side to open the gap again. Her only option was to keep going and try to find the Crystal Well before anyone else. Maybe she could smuggle it past them while they were searching for it. At least she could take it and hide it somewhere.

Quinn kept moving in the curving passage as it hooked to the right. She soon reached an area blocked by another cave-in. She was about to turn back, thinking she'd missed something, when a flicker of a breeze brushed her face.

At first, she thought it was a cobweb. It took a second to realize it came from the direction of the second cave-in.

She climbed up on the pile that had spilled down into the passage from the roof. The dirt and stone had broken away from the roof and timbers to fill the tunnel. Pieces of the thick timbers used in the rest of this area jutted from the pile.

Pulling herself to the top, Quinn found a narrow gap in the stone a few feet across and only about eight inches high at its tallest point.

Twisting her head so she could see through to the other side, Quinn spotted a large circular chamber. The roof seemed to be domed, although she couldn't see the top from this angle. One thing she could see were the four skeletons in rags lying at the base of the cave-in on the far side. She figured they were the companions of the screaming man Upwood had seen.

She didn't see anything dangerous in the room. She also didn't see any other exits. Maybe the room opened at the top to somewhere outside. With her face pressed to the opening, she could feel fresh air moving past her.

She stared at the bodies, surrounded by dirt and stone. It could have been the cave-in that killed them. The man Upwood had seen could have been partially buried on this side of the pile and severely injured. His companions might have been screaming for help because they were trapped on the far side. They could have died from lack of water and food. The gap at the top of the rockslide could have opened later.

She pulled at the stones around the tiny gap, letting them tumble behind her. It didn't take much work to widen the gap enough that she figured she could wriggle through.

Quinn listened before she went through, trying to slow her breathing enough to check if there was something on the other side. She leaned forward with her ear to the opening and strained to hear anything at all. There was nothing but the faintest whisper of the air rushing past her head.

She pulled her head out of the gap and stared at it. Then she said, "I'm not going to find out what's going on by staying here. I'm supposed to be scouting, so that's what I'm going to do."

The pep talk helped her feel a little more confident. Quinn ducked her head and shoulders and pushed the top half of her body through the gap. Once she was through to her waist, she grabbed the end of one of the buried timbers and pulled herself the rest of the way.

The loose dirt slid beneath her as her legs came past the opening, and she rolled down to the bottom. She landed between the four skeletons.

Quinn froze, fearing they'd animate and attack her or something. When nothing happened, she sat up and slid on her butt out from between the dead treasure hunters. Only then did she look up and take in the ceiling of the domed chamber for the first time.

The first few feet were worked stone with carved runes spaced evenly around the room as if marking off intervals on the circle. It was what was just above the initial layer of stone that caught her eyes.

The carved stone ended, and the rest of the dome above seemed to be made entirely of glass, cut in facets like a fine crystal wineglass. A chain as thick as her arm hung down from the center of the dome, with a long metal arrow or maybe a spear suspended horizontally from it like a pointer. It swayed a little from the air moving through the chamber.

Quinn had been using her night vision, but that had its limitations. She needed to see this room better than just in shades of gray and green. Pulling out her phone, Quinn switched on the flashlight and gasped. The glass dome magnified the light from her phone a hundred times, filling the room with a brilliant glow.

The chain was made of gold, as was the arrow suspended from it. Both gleamed in the reflected light.

Quinn stood and moved carefully around the remains of the four men. She walked to the center of the room and held her phone up so it shone into the middle of the glass dome. The etchings she'd thought were purely decoration in the glass turned out to be the lines that created a stylized map of the world above her.

She took it all in. This had to be what Gemma wanted. It wasn't what she'd expected. A well was a hole in the ground, wasn't it? Still, the magnificence of the space left no doubt in her mind that this was the Crystal Well.

One thing was certain, now that she'd found it. There was no way Quinn would be able to hide this from anyone who made it this far. There was no smuggling this out of here to keep it away from Gemma.

As she stared at the magnificent sight, Quinn spoke aloud. "I wonder who built it?"

"People long gone now. Killed by invaders from across the sea by war and disease."

Quinn spun. Upwood stood a few feet behind her. He didn't glow like a ghost anymore. He looked like a normal, albeit short, person.

Quinn glared at him. "You lied to me. You knew what was in here all along."

"I'd hoped I could convince you to just wait with me until the others reopened the passage. Then you could've escaped."

"Where's your simple miner's accent?" Quinn asked. "You sound a good deal more educated than you did before."

Upwood smiled. "A necessary subterfuge. As was this getup." He looked down at his clothes and they faded into mist, then reformed into floor-length robes.

Quinn glanced at the skeletons. "And them? I suppose you're the big baddie who killed them? The thing I'm supposed to be frightened of? You're just a ghost. A lying ghost, but a ghost all the same."

"I'm a good deal more than that. I'm the guardian of this place, the one who must protect it at all costs until it is needed to fight those from beyond."

Quinn knew this was headed for a fight. If she could stall, maybe she could find out what Upwood really was. She was pretty sure he wasn't a shifter.

She pointed up at the dome. "How's this oversized

upside-down bowl going to fight anything? It's just sitting here gathering dust."

"Do you see any dust anywhere? This place is as pristine as the day it was created. It's the way it was intended to be."

"You're right. I didn't mean any harm. It's just a figure of speech. I'm not here to corrupt anything. I'm here to protect this place, just like you."

"You're lying." Upwood floated across the floor, growing until he towered over Quinn, his shoulders and head extending into the dome.

"No," Quinn said, holding up her arms, hands outward in surrender. "I haven't lied to you. Everything I said earlier was true. I'm the leader of a new Huntress clan formed in Baltimore. I came here because someone else wants to find this place. She's working with a faction of the Fae who wish to see the return of their kin from the netherworld."

At the mention of the Fae, Upwood spat on the ground. He leaned over her and said, "No Fae I know would think of such a thing. They hold all the power in the world. Why would they give that up to share with their evil cousins from below?"

Quinn shook her head. "Things have changed since you were last outside. The magical world has been surpassed by technology." She held up her phone, which was still filling the room with light. "Like this device. With it, I can do any number of things that would seem like magic to anyone from the past."

"Bah," Upwood said, dismissing what she said with a wave of his hand. He shrank back down to his normal size.

"Magic? Like your flying machines and such? I find it all hard to believe."

"And yet here I am, holding the evidence in my hand. I told you, I haven't lied to you even once. I am the Huntress, and a powerful mage is using those shifters outside to dig their way in here so she can claim this place for herself. I just don't know what she wants to do with it when she gets here."

Quinn stopped, thinking about Gemma's mission. What could she possibly want with a giant glass map?

"Upwood, what does this place do? You said it was vital to some eventual battle. I assume it's with demons from the netherworld. What did you mean? Why is this place called a 'well' when it's not a hole in the ground?"

The old man cackled. "You think a well has to go down. Between dimensions, up and down doesn't matter." He pointed at the dome. "This can foretell the location of the battles to come. It will allow those who must fight to plan ahead and be where the demons will strike next."

"It's a gateway, then?"

"That and much more. The Great Mother Spirit gifted it to those who lived here long ago. She told them to protect it at all costs. Thus, my ancestors have stayed here all these years, living in peace with all our neighbors. Then the others came. They arrived in their big boats, bringing people who had no appreciation for the gift of the Mother. Soon after they arrived, our fellow guardians began to sicken and die, spots covering their bodies as they burned with fever."

Quinn thought back to her history classes in high

school and nodded. "Smallpox and measles. It swept through the defenseless tribes, killing thousands."

"My grandfather and grandmother, along with me, were the last of the guardians. We knew we would soon die. My grandmother gathered the last of her strength and coupled it with that of my grandfather, spending it all to give me the ability to remain here until it was needed."

Upwood raised his hands, looking around. "As my grandparents passed, they called out to the Mother to protect the well. She answered their final prayers and covered the temple with a great hill of stone and earth. It was buried and forgotten for hundreds of years."

Upwood slid the spear or arrow free from the end of the chain. The golden shaft and head glowed in his hands. Quinn's supernatural senses tingled at the power within the weapon.

The old man lowered the spear until it was pointed at Quinn. "Now I must cleanse this place of intruders, as I have always done."

Quinn shifted her feet, backing up. She couldn't decide if he planned to run her through with the weapon to kill her or use the powerful magic she sensed around her.

She tried to decide if she could reach him with her Bowie before he released his attack, whatever it was. When an explosion shook the room, Quinn thought at first it was the beginning of some spell from Upwood. Then she saw the look of shock and confusion on his face.

"What was that?" the guardian asked. He glared at Quinn. "More of your companions, trying to break through to this holy place, no doubt."

"I told you, I'm not with them. Why won't you believe

me? I'm the Huntress, foretold by prophecy, or at least one of them. For all you know, I'm the one you're holding this place for. Maybe you're supposed to help me so I can assist you in defending it from those who would misuse it?"

Another explosion rocked the room. This time, dirt and stone shook loose from the rockslide blocking the entrance. Quinn's silver Huntress amulet grew ice-cold as another explosion sounded and more of the dirt around the entrance cleared. The room filled with dust.

Quinn doubled over, coughing to clear her throat. She looked at Upwood, frozen into immobility by indecision.

Forcing herself upright, Quinn moved in front of the old guardian. "You have to do something. I don't know who or what is out there for sure, but I can guess. Whoever it is, it's powerful, maybe more powerful than either of us can face. Is there another way out of here?"

"I must stay and defend the temple." Upwood held the golden spear pointed at the entrance.

Quinn tugged at his arm. "No, you must live so we can come back better prepared to stop them. Is there another way out?"

Upwood stared at her, wide-eyed. Another explosion shook the room, and more of the cave-in at the entrance cleared. He looked at the entrance, then back at her, and he finally seemed to understand her words.

He pointed at the far wall, then pulled on her hand. "I have a place we can hide. I think you're right. We must be careful in light of the powerful magic out there. Come."

Quinn nodded, glad he was finally listening to reason. She followed him to the far wall beneath one of the overhead sections with the carved runes in the wall. Upwood shifted the golden spear to one hand and raised his empty hand palm up, moving it in a circular motion.

A section of the stone wall moved aside and he gestured for Quinn to enter. Another explosion went off, this one much closer. The blast propelled her through the doorway into the room on the other side. Upwood landed on the stone floor beside her amidst a cloud of dust.

Upwood rolled over and thrust his hand toward the doorway. The stone door slid closed again, sealing out the rest of the dust cloud.

Quinn stifled a cough and blinked through tear-filled eyes, taking in the room in which she found herself. A simple pallet rested on the floor in the corner. A bench and table occupied in another. She heard the gurgle of water nearby, too.

Quinn croaked, "What is this place?"

"It is where I live and sleep when I'm not needed to guard the temple." As Quinn climbed to her feet, she started coughing again. Upwood tugged her arm. "If we are to be compatriots, I can't have you dying in here. There is a spring running through these rooms. Let's get you something to drink while I try to decide what our next action must be."

He leaned the golden spear against the wall by the secret door to the chamber of the Crystal Well. Taking her hand, he led her in the direction of the gurgling water until he told her to kneel down on the stone floor.

Quinn bent forward, extending her hands into a pool of cool water. She splashed water on her face and wiped the grit from her eyes. Blinking, she looked around. She was leaning over a low basin on the floor filled with cool, fresh water that flowed in from a stone spout in the wall and ran out through an outlet in the corner of the basin.

She bent forward again and gulped the water, rinsing her mouth out twice before she cupped her hands and drank. She splashed her face one last time and stood up.

Quinn gestured to the pallet on the floor and the table and bench nearby. "I thought you were a ghost. These are very material things for a ghost to need."

"The ghost is a useful guise to discourage most explorers. I don't relish using violence against people, even interlopers into this place bent on abusing it."

"You could have fooled me. You certainly seemed like you wanted to kill me."

"I didn't expect you to find a way inside. Your appearance out there angered me." The old man looked away in embarrassment. "Most of that anger was directed at myself for failing to dissuade you from continuing your quest."

Quinn looked at the wall where the door to the temple had been. Other than the spear leaning against the wall beside it, she could see no sign of it now. "If that's Gemma and the werepanthers, she'll finally have what she's sought. We should make a plan to stop them from using the Well."

Upwood smiled. "They cannot use it. Do not worry." He pointed at the spear.

"You took it from the chain." Quinn smiled back at him. "I assume it's necessary to activate the magic out there?"

Upwood nodded. "At least in the near term, they will not be able to activate the well. There may be ways to circumvent not having the spear. Powerful magic created those blasts, so it might not take such a spellcaster long to find a solution."

"I need to see if it's who I think it is," Quinn said. "Is there any way to watch what they're doing in there?"

"Yes," Upwood said, then snapped his fingers. "I should have thought of that. I guess it's a good thing I decided to trust you after all. You can never tell anyone what I show you while you're in here."

Quinn zipped her lip and tossed away an imaginary key. "Nothing. I'm not telling anyone. I'm here to do the same thing you are. Once that's accomplished, I'm out of your hair."

Upwood moved to the wall near where they came in and once again made a circular motion with his palm extended. Another portion of the wall near the spring and basin moved aside.

"There is a place where I used to watch the ceremonies as a child. We can see who has invaded the temple and determine our next course of action."

Upwood went through the opening, disappearing into the darkness beyond. Quinn realized she still held her phone in one hand. The flashlight was still lit.

Switching it off, the room darkened, but not completely. Several stones around the small room glowed with a faint blue light. After her eyes adjusted to the change in illumination, Quinn ducked and passed through the opening, following Upwood. She was pretty sure it was Gemma out there, and probably Avery, too. She had to see what they were up to.

CHAPTER TWENTY-FIVE

Clark pulled the car into an alley two blocks from the home on Federal Hill and shut off the headlights. "I think we're close enough. If they have anyone watching the street, we don't want to be spotted."

Naomi smiled, letting her fangs show. "I can take care of anyone lurking in the night who might be a threat."

"Let's avoid bloodshed if we can. Gemma has duped at least one local werepanther pride into joining her, but they don't know what we now know."

"We can't afford to tiptoe around this, Clark. Quinn could be in trouble. We have to get in there and find her."

"You've seen her in action, Naomi. You know what she's capable of when it counts. Let's take it slow. We don't want to make it harder on her if she's hiding somewhere."

Naomi started to say something but stopped and nodded. "Fine, we'll do it your way. What's next?"

Clark shut off the engine. "Let's get as close as we can and see if we can spot anyone on guard. Then we can make a plan."

The two of them got out and walked up the alley. Clark reached the corner and searched the street nearby. He couldn't see anyone, but he didn't trust his eyes. Better to get a second look from another angle. They also needed a better vantage on the Fae house about a block down the street.

Clark studied the area and then pointed at the roof of the adjacent row home. "Can you get up there? I think we need to have eyes on the house before we get any closer."

Naomi glanced up and grinned. "Piece of cake."

Before Clark could answer, the vampire leaped and grasped the rain gutter that ran along the roofline. It was nearly twenty feet up, but she'd reached it with ease. She swung her legs up and disappeared over the edge.

He returned his eyes to the street. He could make out the front of the home from here. There was an alley nearby that might give them an access point to the back of the property. He'd come down an alley from the opposite direction when he came here before. He figured it was the same one.

Naomi returned five minutes later. She dropped silently to the sidewalk beside him and tapped him on the shoulder. When he didn't start, disappointment colored her expression.

Clark grinned and tapped the side of his head. "I can sense supernaturals who get too close to me. You should know that."

"Hey, a girl has to try."

"Try harder next time. What did you see?"

Naomi moved up to the corner and nodded up the

street. "I spotted two guys in biker leather lurking in the shadows beside the big house. That's our target, right?"

Clark nodded. "They're probably part of the werepanther pride Quinn ran into. That clinches it. She was right. Gemma is using the captured werebadgers to tunnel under this neighborhood. Any sign of Quinn?"

Naomi shook her head. "You know Quinn wouldn't have been satisfied with staying out here and scouting the outside of the house."

Clark sighed. She was right. "That girl went in to see for herself, of course. All right, I think we can sneak in from the rear. There's an alley that runs to the back of the house. That should be it right there, down that side street."

"Lead the way," Naomi said. "I'll hang back and watch for anyone tailing us."

Clark nodded and checked the street. He accessed his Hunter magic and dipped into the shadows. As soon as he was hidden, he ran across the street and moved along the front of the homes until he reached the side street.

After a quick glance to make sure Naomi was following, he ran toward the alley at the rear of the nearest home. He swept the area ahead with his Hunter awareness. There was an outside chance Quinn had hidden somewhere nearby and just had a comm failure. He knew it wasn't likely, but it was better than the alternatives his imagination cooked up.

That girl drew trouble like a magnet and found her way into the thick of things by default. The fact that she always found a way out of it in the end only made her bolder, not the other way around. No matter what he'd done to discourage it, that streak of rashness had grown even stronger.

Clark checked the alley to make sure it was clear. He glanced back to see if Naomi was there, then he turned the corner and moved up the alley, hugging the wooden fence that bordered the backs of the homes on his right.

He stopped when he reached the edge of the fence dividing the neighbor's yard from the Victorian home. Clark waited for a long time, scanning the alley ahead.

Something wasn't right.

He crouched and searched the darkness on both sides of the narrow track behind the homes. On the left, several detached garages and some small bushes grew right up to the roadway. It was the same on this side, too. The clumps of brush provided plenty of cover for him. He got the sense that he wasn't the only one hiding out here right now.

"What're you waiting for?" Naomi hissed in his ear.

"Trouble," Clark whispered. "Do you see anyone?"

"No, it's clear."

"Exactly. There were two guards out front. Where are the guards on this side of the house?"

It took only a few seconds for Naomi to realize the same thing he had. "It's a trap."

Clark nodded as he continued to scan the shadows along the alley. He knew others were there. He just had to find them.

Naomi frowned. "You think Quinn already tripped the trap, and they're alerted to the possibility of backup coming to help her?"

"If she's been caught, you can bet Gemma will assume

at least you and I are coming after her. All the more reason to rethink this."

"Agreed," the vampire said. "Let's back out and find a different way in."

Clark ground his teeth at her suggestion. He didn't like to retreat. In this case, though, her idea was probably the best option. He raised one hand to his shoulder and hooked a thumb to the rear.

As soon as he felt Naomi move back, Clark turned around and started back to the alley's entrance.

They almost made it.

As they neared the intersection with the side street, five shadows detached from the darkness around them. A rustle behind him told Clark there were others to the rear.

A voice from the figure in the center of the group ahead of them said, "You two picked the wrong place to take a midnight stroll, Hunter."

Clark straightened from his crouch. No sense in hiding now. "I don't know. I heard this was where all the cool kids hung out."

"Don't play with them, Clark," Naomi said. She'd drawn a narrow sword from beneath her long coat. "They should know we came to earn our panther-skinning merit badges."

"I wanted to give them a chance to start running now," Clark replied as he drew his short sword. The silver blades they carried glinted in the moonlight.

The lead werepanther pointed at the pair. "Get them, but take them alive. The mistress wants sacrifices for her rites later."

The four in the lead and the five from behind charged

Clark and Naomi. The odds weren't great. Werepanthers were a tough variety of shifter.

Clark might have been able to take two on his own, but more than that would be hard. He had no idea what the vampire could do, but he was about to find out.

Clark twisted to face those charging from behind, leaving Naomi to worry about the attackers to the front. He brought up his sword in time to catch the first attacker with a slicing blow that cut the hapless shifter open from sternum to groin as he leaped in at the Hunter.

Unfortunately, the others running up plowed into Clark before he could recover for another attack. Despite the odds, he managed to hack the arm of one of the attackers and pivoted to thrust into the thigh of another. After that, their combined weight bore him to the ground.

Beside him, Naomi had turned into a whirling cyclone of silver alloy death. Two of the werepanthers lay on the ground at her feet.

The leader charged in to lend his weight to the attack, which was enough to drive her backward toward the ones who had subdued Clark. Even a turbocharged vampire/Hunter hybrid like Naomi couldn't hold out under the onslaught that followed.

Soon she lay battered and bruised on the pavement bedside Clark. Once she'd been trussed up the same way they'd tied him, both were hauled to their feet.

Naomi peered out through puffy, swollen eyes and smiled. "Looks like we killed three of the bastards. Fewer to kill after we get loose."

"Shut it, vampire," the leader snarled. "You have no idea what awaits you below. The mistress needs sacrifices of power. You two will do nicely to supplement those she already has for her ritual."

Clark said to Naomi, "They must've already nabbed her."

"You'll see who we have soon enough," the pride leader said. "Now, march."

Their captors shoved both of them hard from behind, so they stumbled up the alley. The fence gate at the rear of the Victorian home stood open, and Clark and Naomi were pushed inside the yard and then half-walked, half-dragged to the back porch.

The leader from the alley ran up the steps to talk to a pair of bulky werepanthers standing on the porch by the kitchen door.

One of them studied the captives and nodded. "They'll do nicely. Take them below. I'll go find the mistress. We're still dealing with the other issue down there."

"Was there trouble?" the shifter from the alley asked.

"Another cave-in, and someone said they spotted some girl down there who caused the collapse. I'm not sure I believe the second part. Those stupid badger folk said they spotted a ghost. I think everyone is spooked down there."

Clark caught Naomi's eye. She grinned at him. Their girl was still alive. That was something, at least.

The leader came back down the steps and motioned to the others. Once again, someone shoved Clark hard from behind, forcing him not up the steps as he'd expected but over to the side of the home, where a wide stone staircase led to the basement.

When he tripped on a hidden root in the yard, the shifters didn't let him get back up on his own. They kicked at him and forced him to crawl the rest of the way to the steps and then roll down them into the dark basement.

Clark rolled over at the bottom of the steps. The low-ceilinged basement had a dirt floor. In the center, a shaft opened to whatever lay below.

Two shifters dragged Clark to his feet and pulled him to a wooden platform rigged to an overhead system of pulleys attached to the ceiling beams and connected to a large drum with rope wound around it. The drum had been attached to a small electric motor. Clark, Naomi, and the others moved onto the makeshift elevator. A werepanther near the motor flipped a switch and nodded as the platform descended into the shaft.

The leader pointed to a series of iron-barred cages arrayed along one wall. "Lock them up in there while we await the mistress's arrival."

The shifters dragged Clark and Naomi over to one of the cells. They were left on the dirt floor while the door was closed and a chain was passed through the bars and secured with a padlock.

Clark rolled over to sit up, then shifted until he could rest his back against the dirt and rock wall at the rear of the cell. Naomi wriggled over until she was next to him.

She chuckled.

Clark glanced at her in the darkness. "What's so funny?"

"We have them right where we want them, don't we?"

He stared at her for a second and then started laughing along with her. Given the situation, there wasn't much else they could do.

CHAPTER TWENTY-SIX

Quinn followed Upwood up a winding staircase, leaving his rooms behind. The narrow passage tilted to the side until she realized one wall was the outside of the dome.

Upwood stopped before the stairs ended, then lowered himself until he was on his hands and knees. He bent forward and probed the stone with his hands for almost a minute. "I haven't been up here since I was very young. I'm not sure I remember where the loose stone is."

"Do you need help?" Quinn asked. She crouched beside him and reached out to run her hands over the rough-hewn surface. She had no idea what she was looking for, but she kept searching.

"Ah, here it is," the old man said. "It's much smaller than I remember."

Quinn heard stone scraping on stone, and a rectangular patch of light appeared between the two of them. Upwood leaned over to peer through the opening. There was room, so Quinn slid closer so she could see, too. She stared down through the glass that comprised the dome. It was a little cloudy, but she could see the room easily.

Several clusters of figures moved on the floor below. A group of the werebadger miners had been herded against the wall by some of the werepanther guards. Several groups of werepanthers moved around the walls, searching for something. Some of them had miner's picks and shovels and tapped on the stone, listening for something as they moved around the perimeter.

Quinn realized they were searching for her. They had seen her through the gap before the other cave-in. They knew there wasn't another way out of the chamber, so they were looking for the way she'd escaped.

"What if they find the door you opened?" she asked Upwood.

"They will not. It requires specific magic to open that portal, even if they somehow detect the room beyond."

"What's to keep them from blasting their way in? If they figure out there's a room on the far side, they're sure to try. That's how they got in here."

From the alarmed expression on Upwood's face, he hadn't considered it.

"I must go down and prepare a reception in case that happens. You may remain here. You'll be safe if you stay hidden."

Quinn nodded and leaned over to stare down into the circular room below. Upwood left and descended back to his room below.

She stared through the narrow window as the bikers searched the walls for hidden doors and passages. A few minutes later, Gemma marched into the room. Avery and another half-dozen werepanthers followed. Two pairs of big shifters carried large burlap bundles. From the shape, they might be captured prisoners, but Quinn couldn't tell for sure.

As Gemma moved to the center of the room, she pointed at the wall by the clustered werebadgers. "Put them over there."

The four werepanthers heaved the two bundles onto the stone floor. A groan escaped from one, telling Quinn her earlier guess had been right.

A shout of triumph drew her attention back to Gemma. The mage stood in the center of the room and raised her arms high overhead, turning in place beside the end of the golden chain.

Gemma laughed. "All these years, I've strived to find this place, Avery. All the time I spent training you culminates tonight."

"I don't understand, Gemma," the new Huntress said. "You still haven't told me why we are down here. What is this place?"

"It's a holy place of power, one of the few that can be used for both light and dark purposes. It will be instrumental in beginning the ascendance of our patron."

"We came here to America to find this place?" Avery pointed at the two sacks. "Who's in there, Gemma? Why did you go to the trouble of bringing them along?"

Gemma frowned. "So many questions, my dear. You never acted this way before you came here. It's that wicked girl and her pseudo-Hunter ideas, I suppose. Once we find her, we'll put an end to that."

Avery twisted, looking around. "Quinn? She's here, too?"

"Of course she is. That little troublemaker always gets in the middle of things when there's important work to be done. She's only survived this long by luck and happenstance. Her string of good fortune ends tonight, as soon as we find her."

Gemma pointed at one of the werepanthers who'd come in with her. He was the largest of them all and stood a good foot taller than the mage. Despite being so big, he seemed intimidated by her command to come closer.

She waited until he'd stepped over and bowed before she spoke. "Where is the girl your man saw in the tunnel before it collapsed?"

The panther chief glanced at several of his underlings. They shook their heads, and he turned back to Gemma. "There's no sign of her, ma'am. Perhaps Guthrie was mistaken."

"I don't believe that, and neither do you," Gemma said. "His description was too accurate for it to be anyone else."

Gemma surveyed the chamber, pivoting in place until she'd made a full circle. "No, I'm sure of it. She's here somewhere. There must be another passage or a ceremonial room attached to this one."

The shifter leader nodded at several of his gang arrayed around the room. Most had stopped tapping on the walls. Each shrugged when he looked their way.

"My men say there's no way out, mistress."

"Just because your thugs couldn't find it, it doesn't mean it's not here." Gemma turned to the huddled group of weary and emaciated werebadgers. "You there. Which of you is the leader?"

After a little mumbling among the miners, one of their number stepped out of the group. "I suppose that's me since old Griff was killed."

There was a snarl in the werebadger's voice.

Gemma smiled. "Good, you still have a little fire in your belly. I like that. It'll help you understand that I mean what I say. I want you to tell me where the other way out of this chamber is located. Do that, and I'll promise to release the remainder of your friends from service—once they have completed the work I have for them, of course."

The werepanther chief bristled. "Mistress, I seriously doubt those pitiful creatures can find what my men could not."

Gemma held up her hand, silencing him in mid-word. "You're not too bright or imaginative, are you? But then, I didn't hire you for that. These badger folk are natural miners. They know underground spaces like this. If there's another way out of this chamber, they'll find it. It's in their blood."

The werebadger glanced at his emaciated and injured group against the wall. It took him only a few seconds to make up his mind. He pointed across the room at the wall just to the right of Quinn's hiding place. She knew immediately he'd pointed at Upwood's hidden door.

"Excellent!" Gemma exclaimed. She shifted her eyes to the hulking werepanther beside her. "Have your men stand back unless they want to get blasted out of existence."

The mage raised her hands, a glowing nimbus of green

light forming around her fingers. The werepanthers scattered around the room ran for cover.

Gemma seemed almost ready to release her spell when a booming voice shouted, "Stop."

The secret door slid open and Upwood stepped through the door bent over double, then stood up. He'd turned himself into an enormous gold-armored warrior. He clutched the golden spear in one hand. It looked much smaller in his massive fist.

"You all must leave this holy place. I will warn you only once. Go now, before I destroy you all."

His voice shook the room, and dust filtered down from the ceiling. The werepanthers started to back toward the exit.

Upwood held out his arm, pointing the gold spearhead at the remaining Weres until they began moving with their fellows. Only Avery and the werepanther leader stood their ground behind Gemma.

Gemma's face went red with rage. "Enough! Can't you fools see this is an illusion?" She spun around, whipping her hands down in rapid succession, shooting green bolts of magic from her outstretched hands. The magical energy streaked across the room toward the guardian.

The old man brought the gold spear around in time to catch the first bolt. He deflected it into the ceiling. To Quinn's surprise, the glass lining the walls didn't shatter. Instead, it absorbed the energy, spreading the fading green out to the glass around it until it dissipated.

The follow-up bolt surged in right behind the first, aimed lower. This time, Upwood failed to intercept it. The energy exploded against his breastplate in a blast of emerald light. The remaining bolts streaked in, adding to the flare of power.

When the blinding light faded, the giant golden guardian was gone. In his place, slumped against the half-opened stone door, lay Upwood's broken and bloody body.

Quinn stifled a shout. She stared at the old man, willing him to move even though she knew he was beyond help. Anger welled inside her, but she reined it in. They outnumbered her, so there was no way for her to take them on alone. She had to bide her time. There would be no swift revenge for Upwood's death.

Gemma turned to Avery. "See, there are enemies arrayed against us. You must be strong and steadfast if you wish to be my companion in what is to come."

Avery stood rigid and stared at the dead man, her mouth open.

Gemma pointed at the two sacks against the wall. "Bring them here, and fetch me the old man's spear. The weapon holds the key to the power of this place. We'll need it for what comes next."

One of the werepanthers ran over to Upwood's body and gingerly picked up the gold staff. He took it to Gemma, arriving as the two prisoners in the sacks were dumped on the floor at her feet.

"Pull them from the bags," Gemma ordered. "I want them to see what awaits them."

The ropes tying the sacks closed were removed, and two guards reached in to pull out the prisoners.

Quinn groaned. They had Clark and Naomi.

Both had their hands and arms pulled back and bound

behind them. Their legs were bound as well, and their mouths were gagged.

"Crap," Quinn muttered to herself. "Of course, they would come down after me." She glanced at the stairs to Upwood's room. Right now, it was suicide to go down there, but she couldn't let them kill Clark and her mother without attempting a rescue.

"Gemma, no," Avery said. She tore her eyes from Clark's and Naomi's battered forms. "What are you doing? They're our friends. We know them."

"No, foolish girl. They're obstacles in our way, nothing more. You must fulfill your destiny and help me activate the magic here. To do that, there must be blood. Their blood."

Avery shook her head and took a step away from Gemma, who held out the spear to her protégé.

Quinn knew then that Avery hadn't known. Just as she had suspected, the other Huntress'd had no idea what had been going on behind the scenes. As hard as it was for Quinn to admit, Avery was as innocent as she'd always seemed.

Below Quinn's vantage point, Avery took another step away from Gemma, shaking her head.

Gemma's voice turned cold as ice. "Girl, don't make me force you to do this. You know I can. This is your destiny. You must complete the spell I cast with the death of these two sacrifices."

"I-I can't. They've done nothing to us. They're not evil or guilty of crimes. They're on our side against those who would destroy the world."

"You don't know anything, Avery," Gemma said. "Look

at them. She's a vampire. Even worse, she's a former Hunter turned vampire. You think she hasn't killed people? You think she was always able to resist drinking from a living victim?"

"And him." She turned to Clark. "He's almost worse. He was part of the betrayal of the Baltimore clan community. The fact that he alone lived is proof of his treachery."

Avery wavered, and Quinn knew the girl was about to make a decision from which she could never return. An idea formed in Quinn's mind. It was desperate, but she had no choice.

Closing her eyes, Quinn took a deep breath and then slowly blew it out as she counted down from ten. She only had one chance to get this right.

A blanket of calm settled over her, something she'd only had a hint of when Avery had first shown her this.

Reaching out with her mind, Quinn prayed she wasn't too far away for the mind-touch to work.

She searched in the darkness within her mind, but there was nothing there. She took another breath and let it out as she pushed her awareness out farther.

A tiny spark glowed in the darkness. Locking onto that light, Quinn drove her awareness toward it.

Avery, can you hear me? You have to stop.

Quinn? Is that you?

Who else would it be? Look, Gemma's lying to you. She's always lied to you, about everything. I found out why Filippa helped support Gemma as she fostered you and others like you. I know why she brought you here.

Filippa is part of this? How? It makes no sense. She's not even on this continent.

Avery, think about what Gemma wants.

Quinn, I—

Do you trust me?

Quinn pleaded with the other Huntress, pouring her emotion into the connection. Opening her eyes, she stared down at Avery, frozen in place as she warred with herself and what Gemma had told her to do. After a second's pause, Avery nodded. Quinn knew it was in reply to her question. She sent one last message.

We are the only ones in here either of us can trust. I'm coming out. If you trust me, follow my lead. We'll do what Huntresses do. We'll protect the helpless, save the innocent, and fight evil in all its forms.

In the circular chamber, Gemma responded to Avery's nod too. "Good, I'm glad you've come to your senses. Come to me and take this weapon. You must use it to spill their traitorous blood. Once you do that, I will show you what we came here to do."

Avery nodded again and walked toward Gemma. With a gasp, Quinn pushed back from the peephole. She knew what Gemma intended. Once Avery slew an undamned soul, her soul would be tainted, giving Gemma a control of her.

Quinn couldn't wait any longer. She raced down the twisting stairs, still putting the pieces of her desperate plan in place in her mind. She had no choice and no more time.

CHAPTER TWENTY-SEVEN

Quinn hit the floor at the foot of the stairs at a dead run, her Bowie in hand. She pulled up her stamina bar and drew half of her available reserves, pouring it into her strength and speed.

Energized, she reached out to the three crossed ley lines running beneath the circular chamber. Her plan was risky, but it was the only one that might work. There were more than a dozen werepanthers and Gemma out there. She couldn't take them all on alone, even with all the power she could hold.

Quinn charged into the room, racing straight at Gemma, Avery, and the captives in the center. So surprised were the werepanthers and others in the room that none of them went after her at first.

She reached the center just as the werepanther leader broke out of his immobility. He snarled and batted away her incoming thrust while he reached out to slash at her throat with the claws on his other hand.

Quinn dodged, leaning backward as she twisted away

from the attack. She adjusted her motion into a spinning back kick, catching the pride leader in the center of his chest.

The kick launched him fifteen feet across the room and he crashed to the floor in a heap, taking down two of his pride-mates.

Gemma screamed in rage, *"Kill her!"* The mage pointed at Quinn, a pair of ping-pong ball-sized orbs of fire launching from her other hand.

Quinn's amulet seared her chest with an icy warning as its protective magic energized. She followed through after the kick and tried to recover enough to avoid the incoming fireballs.

She failed.

Both impacted against her, striking her in the shoulder and back as she leaped back to her feet. The first fireball dissipated in a wisp of smoke as the amulet absorbed its power. All Quinn felt was a flash of warmth. The second burst against the small of her back in a flash of burning agony.

Doing her best to ignore the pain and odor of burnt leather and skin, Quinn assumed a defensive stance. The shifters, frozen in surprise for the first few seconds of her attack, broke from their shock and advanced against her.

Quinn called to Avery, "Come to me. Together, we can stand against them."

Avery once again held her katana, which had materialized as if from thin air. Quinn had to find out how she did that.

Quinn started to smile as Avery started in her direction.

The smile faded as she lowered the tip of her blade and charged at Quinn.

Gemma cheered as Quinn struggled to turn with her blade to parry the incoming strike.

A split second before Avery reached Quinn, she shouted, "Duck!"

The Huntress dove at Quinn, the sword extended in a desperate lunge as Quinn dropped to a crouch. The blade passed over her head to thrust into the chest of a werepanther running at Quinn from behind.

Gemma screamed, "No. What are you doing?"

Quinn laughed, joined by Avery as the two of them shifted into a martial dance of spinning blades, thrusts, and slashes, taking on all incoming attacks.

Using the familiarity gained from days of intense sparring, the pair worked in tandem. They fended off the initial attacks of the advancing shifters. In the process, they dropped two more.

The pride leader returned to the fray and drove at the two women. He called for his fellows as he charged.

This time, the coordinated attack started to break through. Both Quinn and Avery took several hits, sapping at their strength. Quinn dropped another shifter, as did Avery, but it seemed like each was replaced instantly by another. The werepanthers had numbers on their side.

It was time to try the most desperate part of her plan. Quinn kicked at an opponent, driving him back long enough for her to reach out with her mind to draw upon the crossed ley lines beneath their location. A strip of golden power peeled away, bending up toward her.

Quinn couldn't lose control of the flow now and

ignored an incoming attack. The werepanther raked his claws across her exposed belly.

She gasped at the pain but pressed forward with her plan as she reached out with her mind to touch Avery's. At the same instant, the flow of golden power reached her. Quinn let the power fill her and overflow through her to the other Huntress.

Avery's eyes widened as the energy crashed into her. She spared a glance at Quinn.

The sparkle of golden energy in Avery's eyes told Quinn all she needed to know.

It had worked.

Now they had a fighting chance.

Quinn shouted as fresh energy filled her, renewing her speed and strength. Time for the next part of the plan. Even energized, Quinn and Avery would be hard-pressed to win.

Between dodging and attacks, Quinn yelled, "Badgers, are you not the fiercest of shifters? Prove yourselves now."

Quinn couldn't wait for an answer. She twisted and ducked to the side as Avery's sword snaked past her shoulder, catching an attacker in the throat. At the same time, Quinn slashed with her Bowie, hamstringing a man about to wrap Avery up from behind.

Two more down.

She didn't know how many of the werepanthers were left, but it was still too many for her and Avery to take on.

Quinn shouted again. "What are you waiting for? Do it for Inez. Strike back for honor."

The flow of ley line power had thinned faster than she

expected. Feeding it to both of them had drained the energy faster than Quinn had expected.

Both Huntresses bled from multiple wounds. The raw power still fed them, but when it ran out, they'd drop from the loss of the only strength still supporting them.

Across the room came a snarling shout. All of the miners dropped their picks and shovels, shifting at the same time into their werebadger forms. They surged forward, leaping on the werepanthers around Quinn and Avery from behind.

The incoming attack from the miners broke the circle around the Huntresses, giving them a much-needed respite.

"No," Gemma yelled. "You've ruined everything."

Quinn and Avery turned around in time to see the mage launch the golden spear at Quinn. It flew true, flickering green sparks of energy playing along the shaft from a spell driving it faster than mere human muscle could propel it.

Quinn's eyes widened. She was unable to move away, her speed and energy nearly depleted. The leaf-shaped blade came straight at her chest.

A shove from the side launched Quinn away from the incoming strike. She landed on the stone floor hard, sliding several feet on her already injured shoulder.

After she rolled and somehow came back to her feet, ready to defend herself, she saw Avery smiling at her.

Quinn returned the smile. They'd done it. They'd eluded Gemma's final attack and defeated her shifter minions.

The smile faded as the other girl's eyes rolled back in her head and she collapsed.

Quinn cried out as everything around her came into focus again.

Avery lay prone on the floor, her body rigid and trembling with the end of the golden spear jutting from her back. Miniature arcs of green energy ran up and down the spear's shaft.

Gemma had bolted for the tunnel exit, with a few of her shifters right behind her.

The badgers finished off the remaining werepanthers. The fight had gone out of them, and now they just struggled to get away.

Quinn turned toward Gemma at first, then stopped. She couldn't be in two places at once. She couldn't both pursue Gemma and try to save Avery.

Growling deep in her throat, Quinn ripped her eyes from the tunnel and ran to Avery's side.

The redhead's pale skin had turned gray. She lay in a spreading pool of blood.

Quinn had little energy left, but she had to try something. Laying her hands on the woman's back, Quinn pressed on the wound as she gripped the shaft of the magically energized spear. It felt like she had grabbed a live electrical wire.

An idea occurred to Quinn as she groaned at the pain from holding onto the spear. Instead of fighting the magical energy, she opened herself to it, envisioning her spasming hand and arm as a conduit. The arcs of magic power surged from the shaft up her arm.

Quinn directed the flow of power toward expanding

her stamina bar in the HUD. To her surprise, a new bar appeared titled "Manna." That bar filled with the green energy until she'd drawn all of Gemma's spell from the spear.

She drew upon her new source of power and funneled the flow into a healing spell focused on Avery's still form.

As she let the energy of the spell go, Quinn drew the spearhead from Avery's back. The healing power flowed around the wound, staunching the blood and sealing the edges of the gash.

Then the last trickle of manna was gone.

It would have to be enough. Quinn had nothing left. She could barely hold herself up on one arm as she leaned over Avery. She remained there, gasping for air as if she'd just sprinted a mile. It was all she could do to remain conscious.

Gentle hands grasped her shoulder, startling her.

"Quinn, hon, you've done all you could."

She turned to look at her mother, who was crouching behind her, then twisted back to stare at Avery's still form. How long had she been sitting beside her? Someone had rolled her onto her back.

Tears welled in Quinn's eyes. She looked at Clark as he checked the other Huntress' pulse.

"Is she—"

"She'll live," Clark said. He knelt beside Avery.

"Oh, thank God." Quinn let herself sag backward to lean against Naomi.

Clark looked at Quinn. "I don't know what you did, but it seems to have stabilized her. When that spear went through her, I didn't think she had a chance."

Quinn nodded and looked around. She shook her head. "Gemma got away."

"She'd better run fast and far," Naomi growled, her voice icy with resolve. "Now that we've exposed her, she cannot seek refuge with those who might otherwise shelter her. I suspect she'll run back to Filippa."

Quinn said, "We need to deal with that particular piece of Fae trash. You know that, right?" The last question, she directed at Clark.

The old Hunter nodded. Whatever soft spot he'd had for the princess seemed to have hardened at last.

"Gemma said she has others like Avery out there," Quinn continued. "She can train a new Huntress and come back for another try."

Naomi said, "Don't worry about that now. If she comes back, we'll deal with her again."

One of the werebadgers came to the center of the chamber. "We have seen to those of us who are wounded. We must go and find the rest of our brothers and sisters. They're trapped in cages back at the house."

Clark nodded. "Thank you for your help. You've proven your honor, and we are thankful to count you all friends."

"It is we who should thank you. The Huntress reminded us of who we are and who we should be. We will tell Inez what was done today."

Quinn allowed herself a weary grin. "Tell her we'll come by the restaurant when she rebuilds and pick up our free meal as a thank you."

The werebadger smiled. "I will do that."

He gave a stiff nodding bow and turned away. His

remaining companions, some carrying their fallen, followed him from the room.

Quinn leaned toward Avery. "We need to get her somewhere better than this stone floor to recover. Help me lift her."

Naomi frowned. "Quinn, are you sure? You're still weak."

"She saved my life, Mother."

Naomi nodded, a grin spreading across her face. It was only the second time Quinn had called her that aloud.

Together, Quinn and Naomi lifted Avery. Clark retrieved the golden spear and followed them out, leaving the chamber of the Crystal Well behind them.

They'd have to return. They needed to divine more about its power, which the Huntress must use sometime in the future. That could wait a few days since they had the spear. Gemma and Filippa would need time to recover and plan a new attack.

Let them come, Quinn thought. *I'll be ready.*

CHAPTER TWENTY-EIGHT

A cough from her bedroom woke Quinn. She sat up from where she'd been asleep on the couch. For three days, she'd slept out here so Avery could get the best rest possible.

Quinn glanced at her phone. It was early, barely six in the morning. She stood and padded to the doorway to check on her guest. Quinn smiled as Avery's puzzled expression greeted her from where she sat up in bed.

"Finally awake, I see," Quinn greeted her.

"How long?"

"Were you asleep? Three days. Taylor wanted us to take you to the hospital. I nixed that. I knew your Huntress genes would heal you if we gave them time."

Avery reached around to rub her lower back. "I ache. Especially down here."

"You saved me, but you forgot to dodge the stupid spear." Quinn smiled and walked to the bed to sit beside the other Huntress. "Some might call that an epic fail."

"I remember." Avery met Quinn's eyes as she realized

what had happened. She reached out and took Quinn's hand in hers. "That should have killed me. You did it, didn't you? You found a way to transfer the healing energy, just like I showed you."

"I had a little help, but yes, I figured it out." Quinn didn't mention her hand. It still tingled from gripping the spear while the magic flowed through her.

"And Gemma? Did you get her?"

Quinn shook her head. "She got away. Clark and Naomi have been out searching the city, but there's no sign. The last I heard, a contact told Clark she might be headed south toward the Carolinas or maybe Florida. We're not wasting time chasing her as long as she's gone from Baltimore. She'll come back, and when she does, she'll have two Huntresses to deal with."

"You think she'll return?" Avery asked.

"If she doesn't, I don't think Filippa will be very happy about it."

Avery's stomach let out a long, gurgling growl. The women stared at each other for a split second and then burst out laughing.

"How about I go and make you something to eat down in O'Malley's? There's nothing for breakfast up here. You feel up to coming down, or should I bring it back here?"

Avery patted Quinn's hand and slowly stood, steadying herself on the Huntress' shoulder. "I think I'll be fine, but I need a shower first. You go down, and I'll be right along."

Quinn nodded and watched as Avery headed to the bathroom, grabbing a fresh towel from the closet on her way. As soon as the door closed, Quinn slid her shoes on and grabbed her apartment keys. Time to make breakfast.

If Avery was anything like Quinn, healing energy used a lot of calories. The other Huntress was going to need tons of food to refuel the reserves.

By the time Avery came down twenty minutes later, Quinn had not only pulled together breakfast, but she'd also reached out to the rest of the clan. The others came down to join them. With eggs, sausage, fruit salad, toast, and orange juice laid out on the table, they all sat down to eat.

Quinn said to Clark between bites, "I told Avery you've been out every evening, making sure Gemma has really gone. Any more word from the street last night?"

"No, nothing. Naomi and I have checked every source we have. There's no sign of her."

Naomi nodded. "I think that one tip we got about her heading south was right. Besides, I don't think she'd be stupid enough to stick around. I say she's gone."

"What about the chamber with the glass dome? She wanted access to the magic there." Avery asked.

"It's called the Crystal Well," Taylor said. "I bet Gemma will think twice before she heads back down there. First, Quinn kept the golden spear. Apparently, that's needed to activate the room's magic. Second, Inez and her werebadgers took on the task to act as guardians for the whole place after the original guardian was killed. They've taken over watching not only the room but the entire system of tunnels they re-opened."

Quinn smiled. "If she and her followers show up again in force, the werebadgers should be able to hold the tunnels long enough to sound the alarm so we can get there to take her down. The only thing we have to worry about is whether she really has more Huntresses stashed somewhere."

Avery frowned and Quinn asked, "What's wrong? You're safe now. We won't let her hurt you."

"But what of the others? You're right. If she has more girls like us out there, they're in danger."

Quinn smiled. "It's all right, Avery. We'll keep an eye out for any other Huntresses coming to town."

"But they won't know…well, anything. I grew up thinking I was unique. Since everything happened, I'm confused, just struggling to understand who I am. Thinking of what she could do to corrupt others like me, I'm not sure I can remain here where it's safe, knowing what I do. I have to find them and warn as many as possible about Gemma and what's been done to them."

Quinn tried to hide her disappointment. She'd hoped Avery was here to stay. The two of them might've had a chance at something more than a friendship. "You don't have to go right away, do you?"

"Perhaps not immediately. I need to recover my strength. But I can't remain here for longer than that takes me. I'm not the one and only Huntress like you are, but I'm still trained as one. This is something I have to do."

Taylor asked, "Where will you start? You didn't know any of the others, right?"

"No, I did not. I'll have to return to the castle where Gemma raised me. There must be records there about the others. She was meticulous about keeping track of everything else."

Clark nodded. "If you find something we can use, please forward it to us. Anything we can do to put a hold on Gemma's plans to return will be helpful. We can help, too. I'll reach out to the Keeper, Joshua Dalton. He's been able to locate more of our lost financial resources. We're not rich by any measure, but he should be able to get you what you need to travel there and begin your search."

"Thank you," Avery said. "I will make sure to report anything I find."

"We'll all need to keep in touch," Naomi said. "We will pass along any information we turn up, too. This has the feel of something larger than just this one attack. More information from other sources will help paint a better picture of what Gemma and Filippa are planning next."

Avery smiled and dug into her breakfast, pulling more sausage onto her plate and adding a scoop of the scrambled eggs. By Quinn's count, that was her third serving.

Quinn sat in silence while the others added their ideas about how they could help Avery with her new mission. She was afraid if she said anything, she'd betray the sadness she felt at Avery's announcement.

Once breakfast was finished, they all helped clean up, so Juni and the other servers didn't have extra work. Afterward, everyone headed off to take care of their own duties, leaving Quinn and Avery alone at the table.

Avery smiled at Quinn. "You're not angry with me for leaving, are you?"

"To be honest, no. A little sad or maybe disappointed." Quinn quickly added, "Not in you, never that. But I'd hoped we'd—" She stopped and met Avery's eyes.

"There'll be time for that. I promise. First, we have to attend to our duty. If we don't, nothing we build together can last. You see that, don't you?"

"I do, but I don't have to like it. When will you leave?" Quinn asked.

"A few days, I think. I already feel better than I did when I got up this morning."

Quinn sighed and stood. "Well then, we should start getting the things you'll need together. We can't let you leave without the things every Huntress needs for the road."

"I'd like that," Avery replied. "Maybe we can get in a little shopping before I go."

"Definitely. Come on upstairs and get some more rest. If you're anything like me, after an injury and a load of food, you're going to want some sack time."

Avery shot Quinn a sly grin. "Only if you join me."

"But you said—"

"We have two days, Quinn. Let's make the most of the time we have."

Quinn smiled and stood, taking the Huntress' hand in hers. Two days wasn't much, but at least they'd have some great memories to hold them over until Avery returned.

Want an exclusive sneak peek at a deleted short epilogue? Find out a little of what awaits Quinn next in the upcoming *Huntress Adept,* book 5 of the *Huntress Clan Saga.*

When the time came for Avery to catch her red-eye flight to Paris, Quinn had a hard time hiding her disappointment. Their interlude had gone by too fast, and now it was over.

Taylor and Naomi had come by and taken Avery's bags down to Clark's car, leaving the two Huntresses alone in the apartment one last time. Quinn stood by the window in the living room, staring out the window overlooking the alley where Clark's car sat, ready to leave.

Avery came up from behind and wrapped her arms around Quinn's waist. She let her chin rest on the girl's shoulder. "If everything goes as planned, I won't be that long."

"I know," Quinn said. "I guess I hoped for one more day."

"One day or a hundred, the sooner I go, the sooner I'll be able to return." Avery let go and walked to where the golden spear sat propped against the wall. She brushed her fingertips down the smooth shaft.

Quinn glanced at the dragon egg, perched atop a pillow on the chair next to the spear. She chuckled. "I seem to be gathering quite the collection of rare and magical artifacts."

Avery laughed. "Just be careful. There are legends about what happens when items of great power get too close to each other. You wouldn't want an explosion of arcane energy on your hands."

"Yeah." Quinn laughed. "Don't want to cross the streams and all that nonsense. Don't worry, the egg isn't mine. I'm only watching it for a little while longer. Soon enough, it'll be going back to Aurora, where it belongs."

She realized as she said it that the thought of losing the egg at the end of the year was going to make her sad all over again. Quinn reached out and patted the egg. It vibrated gently under her fingers.

"I guess it's time to go," she said. "Come on. At least I can ride with you to the airport. You'd better keep in touch while you're over there. Tell me if you run into any trouble, and we'll gather the troops as soon as you call."

"I'll be fine," Avery said, starting for the door. "Let's go. The others are waiting."

Quinn nodded and followed Avery out of the apartment. She let her residual angst go as she pulled the door closed, letting it shut a little harder than she had to.

Inside, unseen by anyone, the slamming door shook the room a little. The spear slid from where it propped against the wall to bump into the chair beside it.

On the way to the floor, the spear's blade kissed the edge of the dragon shell. It wasn't much, but it turned out to be enough. Golden light flared in the darkened apartment, transferring from the blade in a cascade of sparks that surrounded the eggshell. The exchange only lasted for a second before the shaft rolled the rest of the way off the chair and clattered to the floor.

On the pillow, the egg rocked violently for nearly thirty seconds while golden sparks shot across its surface. The energy dissipated, and the room darkened again as the egg stilled.

Clark started the car and drove toward the airport. A whisper of someone calling her name tickled Quinn's ear, causing her to turn to find out who it was. Seeing no one in the alley, she settled back in beside Avery, content to enjoy the peace of the moment. She hoped it would hold for a little while.

Don't miss any of the updates in the regular newsletter several times each month. We'll have book announcements, special offers from select friends, and free books to keep you reading until *Huntress Adept* comes out soon.

(Remember, you can unsubscribe from the email newsletter at any time. There's a link to do so at the bottom of every email you receive from me.)

Extreme Medical Services: Medical Care On The Fringes Of Humanity

Monsters, Paramedics, and Street Medicine

New paramedic Dean Flynn is fresh out of the academy.

Then he learns his patients aren't your normal 911 callers.

With patients that are vampires, werewolves, fairies and more, will Dean survive his first days on the new job?

Will his patients?

Come along now with Extreme Medical Services, a supernatural medical thrill-ride with the paramedics of Elk City by best-selling author and real-life paramedic Jamie Davis.

Jump on the ambulance with Dean, Brynne and the rest of the team.

Get the first book in this best-selling service for free at Amazon.com.

As I finished up writing Huntress Scout the world was in the midst of the Coronavirus lockdown. In some ways it felt very strange to write about Quinn and the rest of the clan going out without wearing masks or talking about social distancing. The members of the clan are the type who need to be out in their community, ensuring safety, making sure the bad guys don't get away with stuff.

I'm an RN and a retired paramedic which is why I like to write about heroes and those who go out to make a difference no matter the danger. My characters use their powers to protect them while they vanquish the bad guys and save the day. However, it's important to realize there are real heroes among us who go out to serve their communities without super powers to back them up. They're normal folks just like you and me. They are our mothers, fathers, brothers, sisters, children, and neighbors. They're everyday people who do what they do day in, day out without asking for recognition.

Maybe you're one of these unsung heroes, the "essential

employees" of all kinds who are as scared as the rest of us are of this danger we can't see or touch. If so, I want you all to know I write these stories with you in mind. That's because the real heroes in our world are the ones who are scared as hell and still find the resolve inside to go and do what needs to be done.

We used to think of these people in specific roles as soldiers, EMTs, firefighters, and police officers. But one of the things this horrible pandemic has done for me is to remind me that we all have that hero inside us. We know this because there are grocery clerks and stockers, ER techs, warehouse employees, truck drivers and delivery people, and so many more normal, ordinary neighbors just like you and me who thumb their noses at this virus. They keep going to work so we can stay home and safe while this storm passes over us.

I urge you all to keep this in mind because we're all being tested in this difficult time. When you see an opportunity to let out the hero inside you, release them and follow through. There are many people suffering because they're hungry, lonely, depressed, and anxious. This is the time where a phone call, a FaceTime, a Zoom call, or even a simple text message can make you a hero to someone else when they need it the most. None of us are truly alone when one other person expresses compassion and concern. Remember and be the hero.

Until next time, thanks for reading my books. Peace.

Jamie Davis is a nurse, retired paramedic, author, and nationally recognized medical educator who began teaching new emergency responders as a training officer for his local EMS program. He loves everything fantasy and sci-fi and especially the places where stories intersect with his love of medicine or gaming.

Jamie lives in a home in the woods in Maryland with his wife, three children, and dog. He is an avid gamer, preferring historical and fantasy miniature gaming, as well as tabletop games. He writes urban and contemporary paranormal fantasy stories, and LitRPG/GameLit, among other things.

He loves hearing from readers and going to cons and events where he meets up with fans. Reach out and say "hi." Visit JamieDavisBooks.com for more books, free offers and more!

Author site is: https://jamiedavisbooks.com

Facebook group is: https://facebook.com/groups/funfantasyreaders

Twitter — https://twitter.com/podmedic

Instagram — https://instagram.com/podmedic